Christian Jr./Sr High School
2100 Greenfield Dr
El Cajon, CA 92019

MISSION 8

ROBOT WAR

D0957798

mars DIARIES

MISSION 8

ROBOT WAR

Christian Jr./Sr High School
2100 Greenfield Dr
El Cajon, CA 92019

SIGMUND BROUWER

T 19622

TYNDALE HOUSE PUBLISHERS, INC.
WHEATON, ILLINOIS

Visit Tyndale's exciting Web site for kids at www.marsdiaries.com

Copyright © 2001 by Sigmund Brouwer. All rights reserved.

Cover photograph copyright © by Digital Vision Ltd. All rights reserved.

Designed by Justin Ahrens and Ron Kaufmann

Edited by Ramona Cramer Tucker

Scripture quotations are taken from the *Holy Bible*, New Living Translation, copyright © 1996. Used by permission of Tyndale House Publishers, Inc., Wheaton, Illinois 60189. All rights reserved.

This novel is a work of fiction. Names, characters, places, and incidents are either the product of the author's imagination or are used fictitiously. Any resemblance to actual events, locales, organizations, or persons, living or dead, is entirely coincidental and beyond the intent of either the author or publisher.

ISBN 0-8423-4311-3

Printed in the United States of America

07	06	05	04	03	02	01
7	6	5	4	3	2	1

THIS SERIES IS DEDICATED
IN MEMORY OF MARTYN GODFREY.

Martyn, you wrote books that reached all of us kids at heart. You wrote them because you really cared. We all miss you.

Thanks to all of you for your help with this diary!
  T.J. McClanahan
  Cody Monroe
  John Greer
  Tyler Buck
  Katelyn Ridemour
  Whitney Stafford
  Rebecca Emerson
  Katlyn McClanahan
  Ryan Haskins
  Chris Hamilton
  Jake Monroe
  Dustin Benson
  Casey Newson
  Leslie Wood
  Kelsey Mays
  Chelsea Jeffries
  Britnie Delozier
  Claire Hamilton

CHAPTER 1

Smoke bomb!

The only indication of the explosion had been a small crackle and a flash of blinding light. Instead of shock waves of blasting heat, however, dark smoke instantly mushroomed in the warehouse, blocking all light. And sucking out all oxygen.

Like any human, my body and lungs needed oxygen to survive. As the dense, choking smoke filled my vision, I fought panic. If I weren't seeing this through the eyes of a robot, I'd be dead as soon as my lungs ran short of air.

"Targets! Targets! Targets!" a deep voice yelled from somewhere in the smoke. "Kill! Kill! Kill!"

Weird, high-pitched hissing sounds whined past my microphones.

More screaming.

Something—or someone—banged into the hard titanium shell of my robot.

By the clank, I knew I'd been hit by another robot. Mine was one of nearly two dozen robots in the room. But that was about all I knew.

I'd connected to this robot body only 30 seconds

1

before. Barely enough time to look around and see the small army of other robots.

Thousands of miles away, the nervous system of my own body was plugged in to a computer that allowed me to control this robot through my own brain waves. I had done that plenty—handled a robot—but not like this before.

Because this robot was different.

It rode on wheels, like the one I was used to controlling. But this one was much shorter, with four arms. Two arms ended with the normal titanium hands that I'd trained with my entire life. Two others ended in round tubes.

I had no idea what to do with those tubes.

The weird hissing sounds continued to buzz overtop in the black confusion of the smoke.

"Ten seconds!" the voice screamed. "Kill! Kill! Kill!"

I made a mental command to switch to infrared, something I should have done the instant the smoke mushroomed.

My robot's controls switched away from visual, and the four video lenses mounted on top of the stem of the robot body blinkered shut.

Temperature sensors gave me instant feedback of my surroundings. What I saw in the shades of blue and orange and red was completely eerie.

The smoke roiled in clouds of cool blue, telling me the bomb had not been a heat detonator, nor something intended to explode anything but the smoke. My infrared detected glowing red shapes in the smoke. Human shapes.

"Fifteen seconds! Kill! Kill! Kill!"

Around those red human shapes and me was a frenzy of movement, the faintly red outlines of the titanium shells at room temperature. They scurried back and forth in the smoke. Laser shots zipped from their extended arms, piercing the shading of the smoke.

Laser shots? This was the purpose of the tubes at the end of my extra arms?

I lifted one arm and pointed at the ceiling.

I thought out a mental command. *Fire?*

Nothing happened.

I tried another mental command. *Shoot?*

Nothing.

Kill?

It fired. A weird buzzing sound came from my extended arm. My infrared picked up a hot laser that left a tight red glowing circle in the ceiling.

I was shooting!

"Twenty seconds! Kill! Kill! Kill!"

As I began to orient myself and focus better, I saw that the laser beams were going through those human forms, like dozens of blindingly fast arrows zinging through the smoke.

Kill? As in kill people?

Robots spun and circled in all directions. The human shapes ran or crouched or fell.

More laser beams.

More targets pierced.

But where were the screams of dying people?

"Kill! Kill! Kill!"

I scanned with my infrared again. There were only two remaining human figures. One pushed against the far wall, as if it were trying to claw its way out of danger. The other collapsed as I watched.

"Thirty seconds! Kill! Kill!"

It seemed as if all the robots turned their attention to the red glow of that final human shape against the far wall.

Dozens of laser beams zipped toward the upper body, and instantly the shape fell.

"Thirty-three seconds! And stop! Back to visuals."

A giant whoosh began to roar.

I unblinkered my video lenses. I saw fans in the ceiling sucking away the smoke.

As the smoke lifted and the bare walls of the warehouse began to appear beyond all the other robots, I looked for all the bodies of the humans who had been shot with laser beams.

Nothing.

Where were the bodies?

I had no time to wonder.

A door opened on the far wall and a man in a soldier's uniform appeared.

"Thirty-three seconds! You are bumbling, pathetic fools!" he shouted through pale, thin lips. He had short blond hair, and his arm and shoulder muscles looked like small, smooth boulders under the tightness of his clothing. His thick neck bulged with veins. "Your opponents were totally blind! And you took over half a minute to kill them!"

Kill them? But where were they?

"And you! Number 17!"

He strode toward my robot body, pointing a flashlight in his right hand at me. Stopping in front of me, he slapped the flashlight in the open palm of his left hand.

"Look above you!" he roared. "Two ceiling holes! Do you think the human soldiers are going to fly to get away?"

I tilted my video lenses up to where he pointed. Little wisps of smoke curled from where I had fired.

"Those were the only two shots you fired!" he yelled. Lifting his cold gray eyes off my robot body, he looked around. "All of you!" he shouted. "Each shot you take is monitored by computer! We see exactly what you do!"

He directed his next words back to me. "What, you were trying to be merciful? To simulated computer targets?"

I didn't answer. I didn't trust my robot voice to not reveal who I really was—an enemy infiltrator, not the scared kid this man thought he was controlling. I was just glad my actual body was thousands of miles from this terrifying giant.

"When the time comes to kill, you *will* kill! Hear me? Or you will be killed! One flick of a computer switch and your death chip will be activated. Understand?"

He wasn't asking as if he expected an answer. It was a direct command.

"All of you!" he roared to the other robots. "Let Number 17 here be an example."

He lifted the flashlight high, like he was going to hit me with it. I almost backed away. Then he lowered it and smiled. "Sweet dreams."

He touched the robot's body stem lightly with the flashlight. That's when I discovered it wasn't a flashlight.

I heard myself scream as an electrical shock ripped through my consciousness.

And I fell into a darkness far blacker than any room filled with smoke.

CHAPTER 2

I woke up seeing the world around me through my own eyes, not the video lenses of a robot. The jolt had disconnected me from the robot body. I now sat in my wheelchair, nowhere near the training warehouse or the robot body that had just been delivering information to my brain. The "bot-pack" was still plugged in to my spine.

What I saw was another windowless room, filled with large, clear cylinders that contained a dark jelly. Two of these 23 cylinders were empty except for the dark jelly. But each of the other cylinders held one kid about my age, with the dark jelly holding them in place. Wires and tubes ran from the ceiling down into the jelly cylinders, connecting to the skulls and arms of each kid. Other tubes removed their body wastes. Only their heads appeared above the jelly. Although their eyes and ears were covered with contoured wax, these kids weren't dead. Only unconscious to the activities around them in this room.

All of them were trapped. Permanently. In 24-hour-a-day life-support systems.

These were the kids running the soldier robots. The kids who had been ordered to kill, kill, kill!

"Stun rod," I said. My words came out as a croak. And my head hurt like it had been sent spinning with a whack from the blunt edge of an axe. I didn't even want to think about how many other times I'd been shocked out of robot contact. Rawling McTigre, my friend on Mars and the director of the Mars Project, had promised that low-level shocks like this wouldn't do any permanent damage.

"Stun rod?" Two anxious faces peered down at me.

"Stun rod." Because I'd been born on Mars and had only recently arrived on Earth, I could only guess from memories of all the DVD-gigaroms I'd watched growing up there. "I'm pretty sure that's what happened. He zapped me with a stun rod."

"He? Tyce, who is this 'he' who zapped you?" This question came from the man's face closest to me. It was still out of focus since my head had not stopped its spinning sensation. But I had just traveled with this man for four days. Nate. Nicknamed "Wild Man" by his platoon buddies in the Combat Force of the World United Federation. I knew what his face would look like when my vision cleared.

Four days ago, Ashley and I had been taken off guard by this Wild Man when he'd hijacked our boat in the Everglades just as we were trying to escape from the Combat Force military prison. But after we'd found out Nate was really on our side and trying to help us, he wasn't nearly as scary. And now that he'd also shaved off his big, bushy black beard and cut his equally bushy long hair, he almost looked respectable. Especially since he'd swapped his tattered wilderness clothing for a black turtleneck and tan pants. He said he didn't want to draw attention to us, since we were on the run.

"He. Big he. Mean he. That's all I know about he." I

grinned at Nate, even though the extra movement hurt my face. "Am I making sense yet?"

"Why were you zapped? What was happening on the . . ." The other face belonged to General Jeb McNamee. Nate called him by his military nickname, "Cannon." Years ago Cannon had been Nate's commander in an elite unit of the Combat Force called the E.A.G.L.E.S. I'd asked Nate what that meant, and he'd only said, "We were trained to fly anything, pilot any kind of boat, drive any vehicle. We were experts in things that now give me nightmares." After the look he'd given me, I hadn't wanted to ask more.

"What was happening on the other side?" I finished for Cannon. One of the top-ranking generals in the Combat Force, he was on this secret mission with us.

As he nodded, my eyes could finally focus on him. Nothing had changed. He still had a face ugly enough to scare little children—a square face, bent nose, and shaved head. A large man in army fatigues, he was the kind of guy you didn't mess with. My friend Ashley and I were glad that he, like Wild Man, was on our side.

Even though the general was up-to-date with all military technology, robot control seemed all new to him. I think he was still trying to grasp the concept—and its potential. It was almost like he was still in disbelief that my brain waves could be converted into digital signals that bounced off an orbiting satellite into a robot's computer system. I could understand. I'd only found out I had the capability less than a year ago, on Mars.

"Training exercise," I answered. "At least I think it was. They filled a room with smoke and made all the robots switch to infrared. The targets were . . ." I paused, struggling to make sense of what I'd seen. "The targets must have been simulated by a computer. They were human shaped. With human temperatures. He wanted us to kill them as fast as possible. He was angry it took over 30 seconds."

"What kind of weapons?" Nate demanded.

"How many targets?" Cannon insisted.

I understood their urgency. These were military men. Their job was to stop what was happening on the other side. Only they didn't know exactly where the other side was. Or the real goal of training robot soldiers.

Trouble was, neither did I.

"I was in for less than a minute," I reminded them. "And I need to get back or—"

A third voice interrupted me. "—or *I'm* dead."

This voice came from Joey, a kid my age. Wrapped in a blanket, he sat on the floor just beyond Nate and Cannon. Ten minutes earlier, he, too, had been suspended on life support in one of the jelly tubes. We had taken him out of the jelly tube and revived him so I could hook myself up to his robot controls and see what was happening through his robot's eyes.

Joey didn't have to remind me why he'd be dead. Somewhere in his body was the death chip that the giant on the other side had threatened to activate. We didn't know how it worked yet—only that if the kids in the jelly tubes disobeyed their orders, they'd be killed.

"Go back," Joey pleaded. "Please. If Stronsky zapped you, he'll expect you to recover any time now."

Joey pointed at another kid pacing the room at the side of my wheelchair. That was Michael. We had taken him out of a jelly tube too so that Ashley could handle his robot. She was now hooked to a bot-pack and sat quietly against the wall, blindfolded so she could totally concentrate on her robot control.

Joey continued. "While you're under, Mike and I will answer as many questions for these guys as possible. But if Stronsky finds out you've replaced me . . ."

He lost his voice to his fear. I understood.

If Stronsky—apparently the name of the giant—found out that two of the robots under his control were handled by Ashley and me, he'd activate both Michael's and Joey's death chips. And we would lose any chance of discovering the mission for the robot army. Which meant that those unknown human targets would also die.

"I'm ready to go back," I said. My head still hurt badly, but I had no choice.

Cannon and Nate nodded.

"We'll learn what we can here," Cannon said. "You've got to find out what's happening there."

I nodded in return. To prepare for my robot control, I pulled my blindfold down and covered my ears with a sound-proof headset.

In total darkness and total silence, I waited for Cannon to reset my bot-pack so I could reconnect with the soldier robot that waited on the other side.

The familiar sensation hit me. As if I were falling off an endless cliff in complete blackness. This was how it always began with robot control. Except this time I had no idea how it would end. Or if I would make it back.

CHAPTER 3

How can I control a robot that's in another place? You might wonder. But really robot control is just an advanced form of virtual-reality computer programming.

In virtual reality, a surround-sight helmet gives you a three-dimensional view of a scene on a computer program. The helmet is wired so that when you turn your head, it directs the computer program to shift the scene as if you were there in real life. Sounds come in like real sounds. Because you're wearing a wired jacket and gloves, the arms and hands you see in your surround-sight picture move wherever you move your own arms and hands. Because I've had a special operation, I can take this a step further. My brain can send and receive information to a robot, which can explore a place while my body remains in another place.

As my friend Rawling had once explained to me, primitive robot-control experiments began as early as the year 2000—more than a quarter of a century before I was born. Scientists attached electrodes to the outside of a monkey's skull, allowing the monkey's brain waves to be sent into a computer. The computer then translated the electrical brain waves into a digitized code, and that code ran a robot. When the monkey moved, a robot on the far side of the room copied the monkey's movements. Later generations of robots did not need to be directly attached to a computer—X-ray remotes sent signals to a small computer attached to the robot body.

Why was I chosen to be among the first humans to control a robot?

Because I'm the only human ever to be born on Mars. Eight Martian years ago—15 Earth years to you—my parents joined the first expedition to set up a colony on Mars. During the long trip away from Earth, my mother, Kristy Wallace, a leading plant biologist, and my father, Chase Sanders, an interplanetary pilot, fell in love. Once on Mars, they got married, and I was born half a Mars year later—which now makes me 14 Earth years old.

Part of the long-term plan to develop Mars involved the use of robots—which don't need oxygen, water, and heat to survive—to explore the red planet. However, the scientists needed robots that could think like humans. So the solution was to let a human brain control a robot body.

Blaine Steven, the Mars Project's first director, had decided I would be that first human. After all, the operation wouldn't work on someone older. The implants had to grow into and fuse with the spine. Plus, the Mars Project hadn't expected babies, and Steven found my very presence to be a nuisance. In addition, I was so far from Earth that if the experiment didn't work, it would be an easy thing to hide.

So Steven had given my mom a hard choice: either I'd get shipped back to Earth (and she knew a baby couldn't withstand the G-forces of space travel), or I'd become the experiment. So I'd had the operation. A special rod, hardly thicker than a needle, was inserted directly into my spinal column, just above the top of my shoulder blades. From that rod, thousands of tiny biological implants—they look like hairs—

stick out of the end of the needle into the middle of my spinal column. As my body grew, these fibers grew into my nervous system. Now each fiber transmits tiny impulses of electricity, allowing my brain to send its signals outside of my body.

These are the signals that control a robot's computer. From all my years of training in a computer simulation program, my mind knows all the muscle moves it takes to handle the virtual-reality controls. Handling the robot is no different, except instead of actually moving my muscles, I imagine I'm moving the muscles. My brain then sends the proper nerve impulses to the robot, and it moves the way my body would have moved.

All of this might sound pretty cool. I mean, on Mars I was able to remain under the Mars Dome, yet explore the planet in a robot's body. I once handled a space torpedo called the *Hammerhead* the same way. And I even got to see the world through the eyes of a miniature robot the size of an ant.

The downside of this for me was simple. And hard to handle. I'd been the first to get the spinal implant operation, and it had left me crippled.

The kids on Earth—like Ashley and the others we were trying to rescue from the Institute in Parker, Arizona—had been wired the same way. However, because they'd had the benefit of better medical facilities, they weren't in wheelchairs.

But I had no reason to feel sorry for myself.

I was in a wheelchair. These kids had been suspended in a 24-hour-a-day life-support system and were allowed to live only through their robot bodies. As robot soldiers, trained and commanded to kill human targets.

And they would be forced to live like that for as long as their human bodies supported their brains.

Unless Ashley and I could find a way to help them.

CHAPTER 4

I emerged out of the darkness to light and to sound.

"How was your return to the jelly cylinder, Number 17?" Stronsky growled as the video lenses of my robot opened.

What I saw first were the yellowing teeth of the giant man's wide snarl as he leaned over my robot body. What I heard was the deep rasp of his loud voice.

"Did you like that sensation?" Stronsky shouted. He didn't ask as if he wanted an answer from me. I think he wanted all the other robots to hear. They were lined up beside me, so that we formed two rows.

"Did you like finding yourself in jelly up to your neck?" the giant man continued. "Did you like feeling all those tubes in your body? Remember, your body is trapped there. We'll leave it there forever, unless you successfully complete this mission. Do you want to spend the rest of your life in a jelly cylinder? Do I need to remind you that the system there will support you for 70 years? That's a long time to be stuck staring at a wall, Number 17."

I knew exactly what he meant. If the life support was automatic—run by a computer—the kids in the jelly tubes would be stuck until they died of old age. And if the computer failed, they would be stuck until they starved to death. Either way, it wasn't good.

"If you don't shape up, you'll get zapped again!" Stronsky shouted at me. He was so worked up that spit flew from his mouth. "Again and again!"

He looked up and down the rows of the other robots. "Is that clear to all of you? We have a mission to accomplish, and I want 100 percent effort! You saw what happened to Number 17. I'll do it to any of you at any time. Understand?"

Stronsky's words died to silence in the large, empty warehouse.

Every kid understood. Being trapped for life in a jelly tube was too awful to even think about.

In the quiet, one robot rolled forward, away from all the others.

"Who are the targets?" this robot asked. Although the robot speakers somewhat disguised the controller's voice, making it sound tinny and mechanical, I wondered if the speaker was Ashley.

Because Stronsky was directly in front of me, I saw his reaction up close.

His eyes widened, his nostrils flared with a quick intake of breath, and then he snorted his anger in shocked disbelief that someone might dare question him.

A moment later the anger faded as pleasure spread across his face. "Number 23," he said softly, "did I hear you right?"

His voice grew louder as he slowly spun in 23's direction. "Number 23, did I hear you right? Did I hear you actually ask about our targets? Even after I disciplined Number 8 this morning for asking the same question? How stupid are you?"

It could be no other person than Ashley. She, like me,

had not been here earlier to hear the morning's instructions. She, like me, wanted to know the targets so we could get that information back to Nate and Cannon.

"How stupid are you?" he repeated. He slapped his stun gun against his palm as he walked purposefully toward 23. "Stupid enough to wonder what I'm going to do to you now? Let's see if you like a shock as much as 17. Let's see if you like five minutes back in the jelly tube."

Not to Ashley, I thought. *I won't let him.*

I lifted the robot arm and aimed the laser tube at Stronsky. All I wanted to do was hit the stun gun in his hand. With luck, he wouldn't know which robot the shot came from.

All I had to do was think the word *kill* and . . .

I watched closely, waiting for a clear shot.

Here . . . it . . . was . . . and . . . *kill!*

Nothing.

I tried it again.

Kill! I thought.

Still nothing.

Shoot, I commanded. *Fire. Bang.*

Nothing. Nothing. And nothing.

Another robot arm reached out and yanked my laser tube down.

"Are you crazy?" the robot voice whispered. "You know that the lasers only fire when they've put in their computer code."

This was Number 12. All of the robots had bright red numbers on their body stems.

"I've got to stop him," I whispered back.

"And kill all of us? Jordan and him are both wired to our death chip activators. If their heartbeats stop, so do ours."

"But—"

"What is that noise behind me?" Stronsky roared.

I froze. Number 12 froze.

"That's what I thought," he said, instantly calm again. "No noise. You aren't dumb enough to risk my anger."

This guy was psycho.

He moved toward 23 again.

"Now, my stupid little robot," he said, looking down on the robot that Ashley controlled. Stronsky was a very large man to be able to look down on our robots, which were nearly six feet tall. "It's time you paid the price for your question."

None of the other robots moved. Neither did 23.

"Tempted to try anything to fight back?" Stronsky asked. "After all, you're five times stronger than I am. Your titanium shell is bullet-proof, and I'm only made of muscle and skin. Come on. Try something."

Number 23 rolled forward.

"Death chip," Stronsky said. "Remember? Death chip. Disobey again, and all I have to do is say the word."

If it were Ashley behind Number 23, the death chip would not kill her. No, it would kill the kid she had replaced, a kid who now shivered under a blanket.

Robot 23 stopped.

"That's better," Stronsky said, still slapping his stun gun against his open palm. "Get ready for your medicine."

If she wanted, Ashley could rip him apart. But that would let the people on this end know that she and I had taken over two of their robots. She'd have to let him stun the robot, as if she *were* scared of the death chip.

"Good little robot," Stronsky said. Very slowly he began to lower the stun gun. The look on his face showed he enjoyed the suspense. It showed he enjoyed his sense of control, making the kid controlling the robot wait and wait and wait for the incredible pain of the electric shock.

I wondered if I should step forward and distract Stronsky. Anything to keep him from hurting my friend Ashley.

Stronsky lowered the stun gun, then pulled it back. "Make you flinch?" he taunted 23.

He began to lower it again. Just before I could shout anything, a loud voice reached us from across the warehouse. "No! Enough! I said *train* them, not *damage* them!"

I definitely knew that voice.

I refocused my video lenses on the man stepping out of the doorway. There was no mistaking the round face, round gold-rimmed glasses, and the evil look on his face. It was Dr. Jordan. Who had tried to kill Ashley and me out in space.

He believed we were dead.

I was afraid to think what might happen once Dr. Jordan found out we were still alive.

And now among his robot soldiers.

CHAPTER 5

"What seems to be the difficulty here?" Dr. Jordan asked in an intimidating tone. He walked quickly across the warehouse floor and was soon eye to eye with Stronsky.

I'd first met Dr. Jordan nine months ago, when he and Ashley arrived on Mars along with my dad, who was piloting the Habitat Lander. Dr. Jordan had claimed to be an artificial-intelligence expert, but I'd later discovered he was really a high-up military general. Actually, as high up in the World United Federation Combat Force as you could go. Worse, he'd been using his connections and power to help the Terratakers, a secret terrorist group that believed the way to solve the overpopulation problem was by strictly controlling growth, and putting the elderly and ill and poor to death.

"Let me repeat," Dr. Jordan said fiercely. "What seems to be the difficulty here?"

Despite his gigantic size, Stronsky looked terrified.

I understood. I'd faced Dr. Jordan's wrath before.

"I am applying discipline techniques," Stronsky said, his voice shaking. "You weren't here, and I know how important it is that all of these robots learn to obey instantly."

"Well, I'm here now," Dr. Jordan snapped. "So tell me who needed discipline and why."

"Number 17 decided to show mercy to his targets during a computer simulation of tomorrow's attack. He shot the ceiling instead of our heat figures."

Dr. Jordan turned his eyes on me. It felt like he was looking right through the robot body and seeing me controlling it in my wheelchair.

"I see," Dr. Jordan said. "And Number 23?"

"Perhaps the opposite problem," Stronsky said. "Number 23 was eager to find out who tomorrow's targets were."

"Perhaps we can forgive Number 23," Jordan said with a sinister smile. "I like a bloodthirsty robot. But I am troubled by Number 17. You applied shock treatment?"

"Yes," Stronsky answered.

Dr. Jordan strode toward me. He tapped his chin as he stared at me thoughtfully. "Did you learn your lesson, Number 17?"

Even though I knew the robot's speakers would alter my real voice, I was afraid to speak.

"Answer me!"

"I learned my lesson," I said.

Dr. Jordan let out a loud sigh. "Perhaps now is the time to let all of you know something." He stepped backward so he could survey all the robot soldiers.

"I know all of you have believed since childhood that you are orphans," he began.

All of us except for me. Because I'd been born on Mars, I was the only one among all the kids who controlled these robots not to have been raised in the Institute—back where they were now held prisoners in jelly tubes. But because of my friendship with Ashley—who had been raised with the others before she was brought to Mars for the Hammerhead mission—I knew what Dr. Jordan said was true. Ashley had told me that both of her parents had died in a car crash. The only thing she had left from them were two silver cross earrings. She'd given one of them to me as a symbol of our friendship.

"In one way, it does make sense that we would use orphans for these robot experiments," Dr. Jordan continued. "Who cares about you? Who would come looking for you? The secret military arm responsible for the operations that gave you robot control would naturally pick experimental test subjects who have no family ties."

Dr. Jordan paused for dramatic effect. "So let me give you some good news. We have lied to you from the beginning. Your parents are not dead."

A low, excited buzzing filled the warehouse. It took me a moment to realize it was the voices of all the robots. With the exception of Ashley and me, the kids who controlled them were each stuck in their jelly tubes back at the Institute. There, even though they were inches apart, they were on life support and could not communicate by the use of their human voices and human ears. The only life they now led was through the robot bodies, and they could only talk among themselves here on this side. Now they were acting no differently than if they had gathered in a schoolyard.

"Silence!" Dr. Jordan roared. "Silence!"

The buzzing and talking instantly stopped.

"Let me now give you the bad news," he said softly. His voice carried clearly. All the others, I guess, were as afraid of him as I was. "Yes, your parents are alive. For now."

The silence seemed to become even more silent—if that were possible—as all of the kids controlling the robots listened intently through the robot audio controls.

"Yes, we can kill you through the death chip. All of you

knew that going into this little military exercise. But now you need to know something more. We can—and will—also kill your parents if you disobey. And your brothers and sisters. Wherever they are in the world."

Dr. Jordan rubbed his goatee as he stared at the robots gathered in front of him. "Think of yourselves as valuable hostages. Your parents are all in positions of power, and they are held helpless because they are afraid of us hurting you. But now you must think of your parents as hostages and fear us hurting them. Wonderful, is it not, how we get so much use out of you?"

The silence remained.

"Good," he said. "Very good that all of you are wise enough not to comment. I expect then that my commands will be obeyed instantly and without question."

He pointed to the open door at the far end of the warehouse. "All of you will follow me. The first one to make any noise will be immediately punished by Stronsky."

Without looking to see if he was being followed, Dr. Jordan spun on his heels and walked toward the door. Stronsky stepped in behind him.

I rolled into line behind the other robots.

Like the perfect army, we followed.

And that was what was most terrifying of all.

For the first time in the history of mankind, we *were* the perfect army.

Undefeatable.

CHAPTER 6

I have never seen a real praying mantis—only a picture of one on the DVD-gigaroms that showed me everything I knew about Earth before I actually got here. In a way, I think our army of robots must have looked like a line of those stick insects. Except, of course, for the lower half, which had an axle that connected two wheels. Turning the robot was simple. If one wheel moved forward while the other moved backward, it could spin instantly.

The robot's upper body, however, did look like a praying mantis. It was sticklike, with a short, thick, hollow pole that stuck upward from the axle. A heavy weight counterbalanced the arms and head. Within this weight was the battery that powered the robot, with wires running up inside the hollow pole to the head parts.

I was familiar with my own robot, the one I had trained with on Mars. I assumed these were based on a nearly identical design, except for the extra two arms that fired the lasers.

I knew that robots were perfect for exploring Mars. But it wasn't until now that I realized robots also made perfect soldiers.

They were strong—their titanium hands could grip a steel bar and bend it.

They were fast—their wheels moved three times faster than any human could sprint.

Bullets wouldn't stop them. Smoke or poison gas wouldn't stop them. Bombs wouldn't kill them. Not with the kids controlling them hundreds or thousands of miles away.

The big question was very simple.

What did Dr. Jordan intend to do with this perfect army?

"Into the truck," Dr. Jordan commanded.

For five minutes we had followed him and Stronsky down a brightly lit corridor. The only noise had been the sound of our wheels squeaking against the floor.

At the end of the corridor Dr. Jordan had pushed a button and a large door had slid open.

It was dark beyond, but after my vision adjusted, I realized it was the inside of a truck trailer, backed up to the warehouse.

"No talking," he said as we filed past him. "None. Not even a whisper."

It was an unnecessary warning. I would have guessed that all of the kids were thinking about what they had just learned.

Their parents were still alive.

Ashley hadn't talked about it much, but it was easy to imagine how often she would have wondered what it might be like to grow up with a real family. I wondered what she was thinking now, knowing her parents *were* alive. Knowing Ashley and how responsible she felt for this mission, I figured she'd shove that news to the back of her mind until we'd rescued the other kids and stopped Dr. Jordan.

Their parents are still alive. If these kids did something wrong with their robots, though, their parents might die.

I understood that too.

Although my mother was still under the dome on Mars, my own father was here on Earth. In a Combat Force prison. Waiting for Ashley and me to rescue him.

I couldn't make mistakes either, or I would lose him, just as surely as if Dr. Jordan had him killed.

I rolled onto the truck with the other robot soldiers.

"Face me," Dr. Jordan ordered from the inside of the warehouse.

Each of us spun our robot bodies quickly.

"Good, good," he said. "See what a little incentive will do for you?"

No one answered.

"We're going to shut the trailer door now," he continued. "Don't worry about getting bored during your trip."

Dr. Jordan took a small remote control out of his pocket. He pressed a button on it and cocked his head as he listened for a beep that told him the signal had been sent successfully.

I wondered where. But when I heard his next words, I understood. It controlled the computers back at the Institute.

"Sleep time, boys and girls," Dr. Jordan said, "A long sleep. Until the day after tomorrow, which is going to be a big day."

Sleep time.

We knew from Michael and Joey that the computer controlling the life-support system sent sleeping drugs into the kids' bodies through the nutrient tubes hooked up to them. The kids fell asleep instantly in their jelly tubes when the drugs hit. It was like shutting them off. In the morning, different drugs would be pumped in to wake them up. It was sad. The kids controlled machines, and yet their bodies had been turned into machines. Dr. Jordan could make them sleep as long as he wanted, then wake them up at his convenience.

It really made me angry that the kids were so helpless. After all, Dr. Jordan was manipulating them, controlling everything about their lives. Making them prisoners in these jelly tubes. And he was doing it all through fear. It wasn't right. Because I knew who was really in charge of the world, and it wasn't Dr. Jordan. But still, how could God—the God I had discovered on Mars and was learning more about on Earth—allow this guy to get away with it? Messing with all these lives? I didn't know the answer, but I had to trust that God knew what he was doing. Someday I'd ask him about it.

It helped that Ashley and I at least had one secret weapon against Dr. Jordan. Because Ashley and I weren't hooked up to the nutrient tubes, we wouldn't be sleeping.

As the door to the truck trailer began to slide down, Dr. Jordan turned to say something to Stronsky.

I amplified the hearing controls of the robot's audio. Above the suddenly loud squeaking of the closing door, I clearly heard their conversation.

"Numbers 17 and 23 were our best students," Dr. Jordan said. "I'm very puzzled that you had problems with them."

"They won't make trouble anymore," Stronsky said. "Nothing like a good shock to—"

"Go easy on the shock treatment," Dr. Jordan interrupted sharply. "These kids are worth billions each. They are irreplaceable as military weapons. We must do nothing

to endanger their lives. I want you to check them out immediately."

"Check them out? They're in the trailer with—"

"Not the robots, idiot. The kids themselves. Run a satellite check and monitor their bodies. I want to make sure all
of their body functions are fine."

If a robot body had blood, mine would have frozen.

I knew what Dr. Jordan didn't. Back on the other side,
two of the kids were not on life support anymore. The computer monitor would pick up no vital signs from either of
them. Once Dr. Jordan discovered this, he'd have some
serious questions about exactly who was controlling the
robot bodies of 17 and 23.

"Ashley!" I hissed into the darkness. Her robot was
somewhere among the others packed into the back of this
truck. "Ashley!"

"Tyce?"

"We have to go back," I said. "Now!"

CHAPTER 7

Ashley beat me back. More accurately, she was quicker than I was in removing her blindfold and headset. For each of us, all it took to leave robot control was a quick mental shout of the word *Stop!*

So, as I lifted my blindfold, she was already standing in front of me, hands poised on her hips in typical Ashley fashion.

She flashed me the grin that always made me feel warm. When she tucked a lock of straight black hair behind her right ear, I saw the flash of her silver cross earring.

Nate and Cannon stood behind her.

"What's happening?" Cannon asked.

"Plenty." I explained what I'd heard. "You know they're using a computer to automatically handle the jelly tubes. Stronsky is about to monitor it remotely any minute now."

"Explain . . ." Cannon's forehead crinkled with concern. "With everything I've been learning today, I think I can guess. But I learned a long time ago not to make assumptions."

I could see the spark in Ashley's almond-shaped eyes as she explained for Cannon's benefit. "If signals are being sent from us here off a satellite to the robots, it wouldn't be hard for them to use the same satellite to get information on their end from a computer here."

She was right. Not too far away, back on the helicopter that had taken us here, was my comp-board, a portable computer that folded up inside its own keyboard. It would be no problem for Dr. Jordan and Stronsky to use one like it on their end to check the computer that ran the life support.

"What's to monitor?" Cannon asked. "I mean, how could they know if any of the kids are disconnected from the jelly cylinders?"

"Brain-wave activity?" I asked.

Michael spoke up. "Through our spinal plugs. We're able to send our brain waves out to control the robots, so I'm sure they'd be able to do it in reverse. If the spinal plug is in place, they might be able to read our brain-wave activity through it."

All of us glanced at the two empty jelly cylinders and then the others, each filled with a kid on life support. Michael had been in one. Joey, who now watched us carefully, had been in the other.

"Don't put me back in," Michael begged. "It's horrible. The only thing you can move is your eyeballs."

"There's only a couple of seconds each day when we reconnect from sleep on this end to the robot on the other," Joey said, sounding panicked. "Those two seconds . . . it feels like I'm trapped forever. How can you ask us to go back in and just wait until all of this is over?" Joey began to cry.

I didn't know what to say. If Dr. Jordan found out what was happening on this end, we wouldn't have a chance of stopping him. But how could we force these kids back into the jelly cylinders? After all they'd been through?

"There's something you should know," Ashley said to Joey and Michael. "Dr. Jordan told us our parents are alive." Her voice stopped there, as if she were choking back a sob.

"What!" Joey stopped crying.

Michael's jaw dropped. "Alive?"

"He's using that against us as a threat," Ashley said. "But once we find a way to stop him, we can all look for our parents. Right?"

"He's planted death chips in all of us," Joey said. "If we don't listen to him, he kills us. And if he dies, the chips are activated automatically. How could we ever stop him?"

"I don't know," Ashley said. "At least not yet. But I do know the only chance we have is to fool him into thinking you are both still hooked up. Then Tyce and I can go back and do our best."

Silence.

"Here's something," I said quietly. "We won't have to put you back in the jelly cylinders. Just get you hooked up again."

"I'll do it," Michael said firmly. "Plug me back in."

"Me too," Joey said, although he had to take a gulp of air. "For as long as it takes."

"It shouldn't be long," I said. I knew the kids were making a big sacrifice, going back to their worst nightmare again. "We'll give Stronsky a half hour to run his check on you. But we've got to move fast."

Cannon and Nate rushed to reconnect both kids.

Ashley stared at all the other rows of jelly cylinders. "Tyce," she said softly, "follow me."

I rolled my wheelchair forward.

Slowly we passed cylinder after cylinder. Each cylinder showed the darker outline of a kid's body stuck in the dark, thick jelly, with the liquid pushing against the thin clothing they wore. Clear liquids slowly dripped through the clear plastic tubing that had been placed in their veins. I'd once thought Mars food was tasteless. Now I wondered what I'd ever complained about. These kids didn't get to eat a single meal. All the vitamins and nutrients they needed to live long, healthy lives reached their blood directly through the veins in their arms.

Most frightening of all, however, were the faces that we passed. Each kid's eyes were closed, and the wax plugs quivered as their eyeballs moved slightly, as if they were dreaming. Or fighting nightmares.

I heard a slight noise. It took me a couple of seconds to realize Ashley was crying.

"I *hate* this," she said. "When we were growing up here in the Institute, none of us knew they had *this* in mind for us. They were getting us ready, like cows for slaughter. Except this is worse than death. They can only live through their robots."

I touched Ashley's hand and gripped it. I hadn't grown up in the Institute, so I couldn't fully feel her pain. But I shared her anger and confusion. How could I help her through what I couldn't understand myself? Maybe someday God would be able to explain why these kids had to go through so much pain.

She continued to cry quietly. "It seems forever since I left here. It wasn't bad, you know. We thought we were orphans. We were learning to run robots. And none of us knew why. But while I was gone, they put everyone into these cylinders. . . ."

She turned away and swiped at her cheek. "I feel so guilty. If I hadn't been sent to Mars, I'd be in one too."

It was true. Ashley *had* escaped this fate because she'd been sent to run some secret experiments on the Hammerhead torpedo. One that would have been controlled like any other robot. One that would have given Dr. Jordan and his Terrataker rebels the capability to kill millions. Only Ashley's bravery had stopped him.

"Someone else might not have survived," I told her. "You did. And returned. It's the only chance the kids have. So if you hadn't been sent to Mars . . . if you hadn't crashed the Hammerhead . . . if you hadn't helped us figure out what was happening to the *Moon Racer* . . . It's almost like God planned for you to be here."

Ashley placed a hand on my shoulder. "Thanks, Tyce."

Suddenly, she tightened her grip as I spoke. ". . . Ashley?"

"Tyce," she said, "I don't believe what I see."

CHAPTER 8

Ashley stared hard into a cylinder.

"I don't believe this," she said. She moved down the row. She stared into another cylinder. Then another. "I really don't believe this."

Before I could roll forward in my wheelchair and catch up with her, she returned.

"Ashley?"

"I know all the kids I grew up with," she said. "We all learned robot controls here, hidden away from the world. Most of us arrived here when we were five or six years old. Old enough to remember our parents."

Ashley drew a deep breath, like she was trying to keep herself from crying again. Then she let the breath out. I could tell she didn't want to talk any more about her parents.

"See, Tyce," she said, "I think they needed to take us when we were that young. The spinal-plug operations probably won't work on older kids who have already done a lot of their growing."

That made sense. I knew my own operation had happened before I could remember.

"And if that is true," she continued, "it makes sense that the younger the kid is, the easier the spinal nerves can grow into the virtual-reality control system."

"Sounds right."

"I'm wondering," she continued, "if it's also easier to train kids the younger they are. I was 10 by the time my spinal plug had grown into my nervous system. And after that, it took me a couple of years to learn the robot controls because I kept mixing it up with my own muscle movements."

"That makes sense too," I replied. On Mars, I'd spent years and years in virtual-reality training sessions before anyone even told me I was capable of robot control.

"I was afraid of that," she answered.

She walked forward a few more paces. I followed.

She pointed at the last few jelly cylinders, the ones she had stared into.

At first, I didn't understand. The jelly was so thick that it hardly let any light into the center, where the kids were suspended.

Then, with horror, I realized what she meant. And what she couldn't believe.

Behind us, all of the kids had been close to her age. Not these kids at the end.

"Ashley," I said slowly, "these kids here are—"

"I know everyone in all the other cylinders," she said. "I know all their faces as if we are brothers and sisters. I've never seen these kids before. And they can't be more than eight years old!"

A shiver ran down my spine. She was right.

They did look like eight-year-olds. With faces much younger than the kids in the other jelly cylinders. Tiny, innocent faces with eyes closed.

It made me sick. My anger grew until I thought it would burst. Dr. Jordan was treating these kids as if they weren't even human. Like they were cows or monkeys in a test lab. Using them as slaves to do his bidding. Not giving them even the chance to experience life outside a jelly tube. In the early 21st century, all such experiments even with animals had been banned. And yet they'd still been going on—with humans this time—right under the World United Federation's nose. Worse, the experiment was being run by one of their own top Combat Force people.

I voiced out loud the thought I didn't want to say. "Are you telling me," I asked Ashley, "that half the kids you grew up with aren't here? And that they've been replaced by these younger kids you don't know?"

"Yes," she stated flatly. In the light her face looked a little green.

When we had first arrived in this room, General Cannon had frantically searched all the cylinders, looking for his own son who had supposedly been kidnapped and taken to the Institute. I now understood why he hadn't found him.

"That can only mean one thing," I said, pointing at the rows of jelly cylinders. "This isn't Dr. Jordan's only army."

CHAPTER 9

"I think we wait one hour," Cannon said wearily to Ashley and me. "By then, Jordan and Stronsky should have finished their monitoring. Then it will be safe to unhook those two boys and let you replace them again. We desperately need you controlling robots on the other side. Otherwise we're totally blind to Jordan's operation."

Cannon's face looked older than it had earlier that morning—before we'd found our way into this place in the Arizona desert mountains. As if defeat had taken away his strength. I thought of the younger kids Ashley and I had just left behind us to return to the general. And I thought I understood why he looked so defeated. Another kid. His son, Chad. It must be terrible to think about him trapped in a jelly tube—somewhere. And not to be able to find him or get to him.

"General?" I said. "I remember the first thing you did when we got here. You looked for your son. You asked Michael and Joey about him."

Cannon nodded slowly. "I was hoping so much I'd find him here. . . ."

Some things were slowly beginning to make sense. Dr.

Jordan had said all the parents of these kids were in positions of power, so that the kids could be used as hostages. Cannon was in a high position in the Combat Force. And no one in government held a higher position than the Supreme Governor of the World United Federation, who had sent Cannon to help Ashley and me. And he was missing his grandson, Brian.

"I'm not sure if this is good news or bad news," I said. "But your son may be in another group."

"Like this?" Cannon's eyes widened.

"I don't know if that group is in jelly cylinders like this one," I replied, "but it's beginning to look like these aren't the only kids with robot control."

Once, not very long ago, I'd thought I was the only kid in the solar system wired to handle a robot. Later I'd thought Ashley was the only other kid. Then I'd learned about an entire Institute of kids like us on Earth. So now it didn't seem so impossible that there could be more than one group.

When I paused, Ashley quickly explained that half the kids in these jelly cylinders were strangers to her.

"You're saying that part of this group has been sent away, with replacements added?" the general's voice boomed. "That there are more than 24 kids with robot control?"

Ashley nodded. "So maybe your Chad is among them."

"But how many groups can there be?" Nate said. He had been pacing in small circles around us, listening intently. "Each one of them might be equipped as an army, just like this one."

"I'm afraid Jordan had access to substantial amounts of funding," Cannon said, shaking his head. "He was one of the top robot scientists in the Combat Force. We all thought . . ."

Cannon put his face in his hands. He sighed as he rubbed his hands back and forth. "It's no coincidence that I'm here," he said. "Since we've got to wait anyway, we've got time for me to explain Earth politics."

We listened. Some of it I knew. Some of it was new to me.

Twenty years earlier, the mushrooming population of the Earth had made it obvious that horrible things were ahead for mankind. Countries were on the verge of war in their desperate search for enough water and energy. All the statistics and research showed that a threshold of efficiency had been reached. Within a century all the available resources would not be enough to support the projected population, let alone continued growth. A third world war was inevitable. With nuclear weapons available to most countries, it would be a war that might cause human extinction.

While many solutions were proposed, only two became popular. And these two caused a growing political divide.

One side called for expansion beyond Earth. Instead of limiting population, they said we should find new places for humans. Like the Moon, where a small colony had already been established under domes. And on Mars, where the dream was to make an entire new planet available for people to live outside of domes.

The other side called for drastic reduction of growth. Instead of spending valuable resources to find room for more people, they said we should limit the population and raise the quality of life.

The most difficult issue was a simple phrase: *drastic reduction of growth.* Which meant proposed solutions like a lottery for licenses that would allow parents to have children. And putting to death "undesirable" people who were disabled, terminally ill, or simply too old. In a Terrataker world, someone like me might simply be eliminated.

As the issue was debated and voted upon, country after country rejected mandatory population control, because that meant allowing government decision makers to play God with people's lives. The choice was made to find new places for people to live, which would only be possible if all the countries in the world joined in this common goal.

This began the next major political debate. World leaders sought a way to make a common political goal possible, without any country losing independence. In the end, the former United Nations became the World United Federation. A 100-year treaty was enacted among all the countries of the world, with a common pledge of resources and technology to the goal of space expansion.

This was not a one-world government, however, with a common currency and one leader. No, the political structures within each country remained unchanged. Each country elected and sent one governor to the World United Federation Summit, which met twice yearly to promote continued peace and the urgent long-term goal of the treaty.

This established the commitment of the world to the Mars Dome.

Yet the highly passionate debate over expansion versus population control left a ticking time bomb within this new world political structure. It was costing billions to support the Mars Dome, and many were angry about the higher taxes needed for this. Within each country, some of the fiercest opponents of space expansion banded together.

They called themselves *Terratakers,* for all they wanted was the Earth alone. And the right to choose who should live and die. As a political group, they made trouble, often. But when it became apparent that they could not change the resolve of the majority by democratic means, they turned to terrorism.

CHAPTER 10

"Terrorism," I said, echoing Cannon's last words. I'd nearly died in space because of that terrorism. And before that, I had seen the results on Mars.

"Terrorism." General Cannon repeated solemnly. "And among that, kidnapping." His voice dropped. "But not highly public kidnappings for ransom. Secret kidnappings. Over a period of years, they took children of men and women who had influence in the government and military. Even those parents didn't realize the kidnappings had taken place."

"I don't understand," I said. "How—"

"I thought my Chad had drowned in a boating accident," the general said. "The river was searched for days, and all the experts said we shouldn't expect to find his body. We had a funeral for him. It was one of the most difficult days of my life. And then . . ."

Cannon's voice broke. "I'll never forget the man's face that day in D.C. So ordinary, like any other person stopping me on the street to ask for directions. But there was something horrible in his eyes that chilled me. He asked if I'd ever like to see my son again. Before I could even begin to show my anger at his disrespect for our family's grief, he held up a photo, with my son holding that day's newspaper. Then he told me the rest."

Cannon drew a breath. "I imagine it's what all the other parents were told. If I let anyone else know Chad was alive, even my wife, they would kill him. Same thing if I let anyone know he was being held hostage. Or if I searched for him. He told me my son was safe and growing up well protected, and that it would stay that way. He promised I would see my son in a couple years, and in the meantime, someone might occasionally ask me for a favor. He said if I wanted my son to live, I'd be wise to give that favor. Then the man walked away and disappeared in the crowd on the street. That was it."

Cannon lifted his hands with a helpless shrug. "What could I do? Too little. I'm one of the highest-ranking Combat Force generals, and I was as powerless as a baby to help my little boy. Then I heard about a senator on the other side of the country whose daughter wandered away in the woods during a picnic and was never found. And about a governor of a country in Africa who had a son taken by a lion, but the body was never found. And someone from Russia who had a son and daughter die in a fire, but the police were unable to identify any remains. Each of them had been extremely pro-Mars, and suddenly each, in their own political systems, began voting against money for the dome. That told me a lot. Even then, with my suspicions, I didn't dare ask questions or begin to look for my son in any way. I couldn't even tell my wife our son was alive, even though she was sick with grief."

Cannon stopped for a long time, staring at the far wall.

"The favor . . . ," Nate said.

"Favor?"

"Did anyone ever come to you?"

"Yes," Cannon said dully. "T.F.T. Tactical Future Technology. A top secret research program. I report directly to the president of the United States. Two years ago, when it looked like funding was going to run dry for T.F.T., I received a note that told me to make sure the money continued to flow for it and to petition the president for it. And I'm talking billions of dollars unknown to the public. I guess they knew I was upset at how some things had gone wrong since I first helped begin that same program."

Cannon snorted bitterly. "After all, when a little-known scientist had first approached me with the idea, I'd been one of the first to see the potential of this new technology. And the first to convince our country's president he should go to the Federation's Supreme Governor to create the secret Tactical Future Technology program. You see, after the prolonged political battles with the Terratakers about mandatory population control, it was obvious the public would be against trying experiments on humans that had only worked on monkeys. But I thought this robot technology would be used for space exploration."

"General?" Nate prompted when Cannon lapsed into silence again.

Cannon's lips were tight with anger as he spoke. "That was 14 years ago. Because of my military ranking, the president listened to me. The dome had been established on Mars, and the second spaceship was about to leave Earth. Because of me, the President and the Supreme Governor arranged for a neural specialist to be on that ship. His assignment was to perform an operation on someone on Mars. An operation that had never been performed on any human. Mars was perfect. We could control the information that reached Earth. And . . ."

In a flash, I knew what he was going to say. So I finished it for him. ". . . and it just so happened that there was one person on Mars young enough that the bioplastic fibers implanted into his spinal column would have a chance to fuse as he grew."

Cannon looked directly at me. "I had the best intentions, Tyce," he said to me with great sadness. "They told me the operation would not fail. That they had performed it on hundreds of monkeys. But they didn't tell me that all those operations had taken place in a controlled environment, with teams of doctors surrounded by millions of dollars of technology. On Mars, when something went wrong . . ."

Again, Cannon couldn't finish his sentence. I was in my wheelchair, directly in front of him. That said enough about what had happened during the operation.

I felt my anger growing. This was the man who had made an order that changed my life forever. Who had given him that right?

Cannon found the strength to mock himself with a smile. "In a real way, I've already been punished. Because that little-known scientist who first approached me put the secret T.F.T. money into research places we nor anyone else in the highest level of government ever expected."

He lifted his arms, taking in the jelly tubes that surrounded us. "Like this."

One last sigh from the general. "In a way, I got the punishment I deserved. My son was taken from me by people paid with money that I had convinced our president to approve on the T.F.T. Because that little-known scientist was Dr. Jordan. We sent him to Mars, posing as an artificial-intelligence expert. But he was the founder of robot control technology. And I discovered far, far too late that he was secretly on the side of the Terratakers."

CHAPTER 11

With Cannon beside me, I wheeled into the cool air of an evening in the desert mountains. The helicopter that had brought us here was parked ahead on flat, packed ground. Behind us, in the sheer rock face of this hidden Arizona valley, was the doorway that led to the rooms of the Institute. And above, the stars pierced the growing darkness of the sky, filling me with a longing for Mars, unreachable all those millions and millions of miles away.

I thought of Mom and the experiments she was doing to find a way to grow plants that could live on Mars. I wondered how she'd react when she found out it was this man who had pushed the funding that put me in a wheelchair. I knew she would tell me to soften my anger at him, something I didn't want to do. I wanted to tell her all the other things that had happened to me on Earth. How beautiful it was. How scared I was with Dad in prison, waiting for Ashley and me to return.

I realized I was homesick. For Mars and for all my memories of growing up under the dome. I would only get there again with my dad if, somehow, Ashley and I found a way to stop Dr. Jordan.

Cannon said nothing as we crossed the short distance to the helicopter. Maybe he was wondering, too, how we might stop Dr. Jordan. More likely, Cannon was angry that we were headed back to the helicopter.

"I don't like this," he said, breaking his silence as we neared the helicopter. "I don't like that you won't tell me why you want to do this. I don't like the way you've given me no choice."

Part of it was because of my anger. I was taking silent satisfaction in pushing him around.

But I had another reason for forcing him to listen to me.

A few minutes ago—right after he'd told us about his involvement with Dr. Jordan—I had asked for the general's password to his E-mail account and access to the Internet through the helicopter's computer system. When I refused to tell him why, Cannon had said no. So I had informed him that, unless he allowed it, I would not handle the robot on the other side for him. I had been bluffing, of course. Along with everything else, my dad's life depended on Ashley's and my success.

"Last chance," Cannon barked as we stopped at the helicopter. "Why are you doing this? Do you have any idea what you are asking to be able to be on my E-mail account?"

"Sir," I said, stone-faced, "I've already explained. I'll be able to tell you later."

He stared at my face and must have seen that I wouldn't change my mind.

"Grunt," Cannon shouted upward to the helicopter pilot, "help us on board." Then he turned to me and spoke softly, "Don't forget that I've already explained something to you too. One simple fact. We don't have much time."

I didn't need the reminder.

From: "General Jeb McNamee"
<mcnameej@combatforce.gov>
To: "Rawling McTigre" <mctigrer@marsdome.ss>
Sent: 03.30.2040, 10:31 P.M.
Subject: Please read this right away!

Rawling, even though this E-mail is coming from General McNamee, it's me. Tyce. Here's how you can know: On the trip you and I and Dad made from the dome to search for the evidence of an alien civilization, I bumped the robot's head underneath the platform buggy as I was trying to fix the flat tire. Remember? And I asked you what kind of pill to take for a robot headache. It was a dumb remark, but Dad was outside in his space suit, so only you and I would know about it.

You're probably wondering why I need to prove it's me. And how and why I've logged on to the E-mail account of a general in the Combat Force of the World United Federation.

Here's the "why" first. It's because I'm not sure you've received any of my E-mails since I left Mars. I'm also not sure if any of the E-mails you sent me actually came from you.

I can't give you all the details now, but you know that I always keep a diary of things that happen to me. With this E-mail, I'll be attaching my diary of the entire trip from Mars to Earth in the Moon Racer and you'll learn about the last person you would have ever suspected to be helping the Terratakers.

The short story is that he was able to secretly access the mainframe computer under the dome. From the time the dome was established! That meant he was able to monitor and change all incoming and outgoing reports and E-mails from Mars to Earth and from Earth to Mars. Most of what you reported about the genetic experimentation, alien civilization, and the Hammerhead space torpedo didn't even reach Earth. We only thought it did, because of the fake E-mails sent back to the dome.

I stopped and thought of Rawling reading this in his office. He'd probably be sitting forward, leaning toward the computer screen in shock, instead of his usual feet-propped-up-on-the-desk habit. I could just see him—his short, dark hair streaked with gray, his wide shoulders that showed he used to be a quarterback on Earth. Although he was in his mid-forties, he was one of my best friends and one of two medical doctors under the dome.

I could just see his office too. I smiled. It was the only one under the dome that had framed paintings of Earth scenes, like sunsets and mountains, on the walls. Rawling hated them, because of what they represented. Blaine Steven, the previous director, had spent a lot of the government's money to get those luxuries included in the expensive cargo shipped to Mars. I bet Rawling still hadn't gotten around to taking them down yet. He always had more pressing matters, like all the life-and-death crises we'd been faced with on Mars recently.

What Rawling might not know yet was that the communications had been controlled from Mars since the beginning. So we on Mars would only get the information that Dr. Jordan and the other Terrataker rebels wanted us to have. And so even the highest-level World United Federation leaders on Earth would only have select information about Mars.

It was incredibly simple and incredibly smart to control all the outgoing and incoming messages and reports on the dome. After all, with Mars 50 million miles from Earth, those communications were the only way to stay in touch. We had no way of knowing that any reports reaching us were lies. And vice versa, with the stuff being sent back to Earth. Who knew how much damage the Terratakers had done this way?

I thought about it and began to type again.

In other words, you may have sent me dozens of E-mails, and I wouldn't know it if someone intercepted them and wrote back as if he were me. Same with the messages I sent you.

I know that to be true because in one of my E-mails I tested you by making a mistake on purpose, and it wasn't corrected. Since then, Dad and I and Ashley almost got fried by getting sucked into the sun, got arrested on Earth after we managed to rescue ourselves, and then were forced to leave Dad behind in a Combat Force prison as we went searching for the other Institute kids. This has been my first chance to send you an E-mail.

I'm doing it from what I think is the safest channel for three reasons. First, to let you know we've made it safely so far. (So far! Keep us in your prayers!) Dr. Jordan found a way to escape, and it will take a complete diary to tell you what's been happening, and I don't have the time. If I get back to you tomorrow, you'll know we stopped him. If not . . .

I lifted my fingers from the keyboard again. We had to stop Dr. Jordan. But there was a big difference between knowing what we had to do and figuring out a way to do it. To me, Dr. Jordan and the army of robot soldiers seemed unbeatable. Especially since he had the power of the death chip to control the kids in the jelly tubes.

Thinking about it, I wanted to give up. But if I had learned anything from Rawling, my mom, and my dad, it was that giving up was never an option.

. . . if not, I don't know when I'll get a chance to send you another E-mail. And that's my second reason for sending this. To let you know that the mainframe computer has been tampered with and that you need to make sure all the communications with Earth haven't been tampered with. (If you don't get this, of course, that means someone else is still intercepting communications, and you'll never know anyhow, but this was the best I could do.)

Third reason? I just want to know that you and Mom are doing fine. I miss you both. A lot. And I pray for you every day. Please send an E-mail back to the general's account, not mine. And please do it right away, because I'll check for mail in a couple of hours. I'll know it's you when you tell me what dumb joke you made in return that day when I made my dumb joke about the robot's headache.

Really hoping to hear from you.

Your friend, Tyce

I saved the E-mail. Then I made a quick copy of my *Moon Racer* diary and attached it to the E-mail before I hit the send button. Although electronic transmissions traveled at the speed of light, it would take a while for the E-mail to travel those 50 million miles and reach the dome's mainframe on Mars.

I wished I could have told Rawling the fourth and most important reason I had sent him that message. But I didn't want to risk revealing it in case someone was monitoring the E-mails.

Right now my life, my dad's life, Ashley's life, and the lives of all the Institute kids depended on Cannon. And yet he was the same guy who had long ago ordered the operation that put me in a wheelchair. The same guy who had been working with Dr. Jordan for years.

Now I wasn't sure if I could trust Cannon. Maybe he had lied about having a son taken hostage. Maybe he was just stringing Ashley and me along with some plan to stop us when Nate could no longer protect us.

It would make me feel a lot better if this E-mail went through. If people were filtering E-mails that went to Mars, one with my name and address would definitely alert them to this E-mail. Chances were, they would let the general's E-mail reach Rawling. And if Rawling replied with the right answer to my question about a dumb joke, I'd know it was him on the other end writing to me. This was the safest way I could think of to reach Rawling, because I still didn't know if the Terratakers had kept control of the dome's mainframe after Dr. Jordan left Mars.

Most important, if the general, who knew I was using his E-mail account, was willing to let Rawling and me correspond, it would tell me I could trust him after all.

And I really needed to be able to do that.

CHAPTER 12

"You want us to what?!?" Cannon said through gritted teeth.

I was back inside the room of the jelly cylinders. Ashley stood beside my wheelchair. Nate and Cannon faced us from a few feet away. The hour had passed, and Cannon and Nate were ready to unhook Michael and Joey so Ashley and I could plug in to their robots. And I had just asked my question.

"Yes, sir," I said calmly. "I mean it."

Cannon's square face was red with anger as he strained to keep his voice calm. "You force me to take you to the chopper. You demand to access my personal E-mail but refuse to tell me why. You take your sweet time and make me wait outside the chopper for you like you're the general and I'm some raw recruit. You don't explain a single thing about it on the way back in here. And now you want us to . . . to . . . to . . ."

Cannon lost his voice. He took a big gulp of air and turned to Nate.

Nate shrugged, unsuccessfully trying to hide his smile. "You heard him, General. He wants us to pinch off all the nutrients in the intravenous tubes of the kids on life support."

"Insane!"

"It's not entirely unreasonable," Nate said, letting his smile grow larger. I think Nate liked being out of the army. He didn't have to jump at the general's every command. "As Tyce pointed out, it's only for a few hours. The kids in the jelly cylinders won't be hurt."

"If you think it's so reasonable," Cannon thundered at Nate, "then make your friend here tell us why. All I want to know is why."

And until I received an E-mail from Rawling and I knew Cannon could be trusted, I was going to tell him as little as possible. After all, as far as I knew, Dad was still stuck in that Combat Force prison in the middle of the Everglades. He was depending on me to get him out. To save his life. Even if it took making one of the highest Federation authorities in the country angry at me, I wasn't going to back down.

"You may have noticed," Nate stated, "when you tried to force Tyce to explain earlier with the E-mail stuff, he proved to be very stubborn. I doubt he's changed over the last half hour."

"But pinching off the tubes. How in the world . . ." Again, the general's voice failed him.

"It should be simple, sir," I replied. "Fold the tube and tie the fold with a short piece of shoelace. That way all the nutrients will be cut off."

"A short piece of shoelace!" He exploded with so much fury that it surprised me. I was glad I wasn't a raw recruit under his command. "Do you see 23 short pieces of shoelace lying around?"

"Actually, sir," I said quietly, "only 21 pieces. Michael

and Joey will be out of the jelly cylinders. Twenty-three minus two leaves—"

"I can do the math!" He paused, and it sounded like he was grinding his teeth. "Do you see 21 pieces of shoelace lying around?"

"Nate has a knife." I'd seen him use it to clean the fish he'd caught for us a few days earlier in the Everglades. That seemed like forever ago.

"A knife!"

"Unless he lost it," I answered.

"And what are we supposed to do with his knife?" Cannon demanded.

I coughed and looked down at the general's feet. He wore high boots, laced tightly.

He followed my eyes.

"No!" he exploded. "No! No! No! That's the last straw! Stay behind then. I'll send Ashley by herself."

From my wheelchair, I peered up at Ashley.

She studied me in return, her serious, olive-skinned face framed by her short dark hair.

Ashley lifted her eyes away from mine and faced the general. "I'm with Tyce," she said. "We both go, or we both stay."

"Nate!" Cannon pleaded. "Help me out here. They listen to you."

"They're not dumb, General. If Tyce wants the tubes pinched and tied, he's got a good reason for it."

"I just want to know the reason! In any military operation, the commander—"

Nate's smile broadened. "I'm not sure who's the commander anymore." He held up his hand to prevent the general from exploding again. "Remember what these two have

63

survived to get here. You could do worse than listening to them."

Cannon opened his mouth. Then shut it without speaking. He leaned over and began to untie his boots. When he had yanked them off, he straightened up and glared at Nate. "Well," he demanded, standing in his socks, "what's taking you so long?"

"Sir?" Nate said.

"Your stupid knife," Cannon barked. "Where is it? We have some laces to cut."

CHAPTER 13

"Where are you?"

"Here," I answered Ashley through the speakers of my robot. We had both just slipped into robot control, leaving behind the jelly cylinders in Arizona.

"Where is here?" she asked.

"Somewhere in the middle." That was the best answer I could give her. The trailer was filled with robots, and it was totally dark. By the loud hum of wheels against pavement and the rush of wind through the cracks, it was obvious that the trailer was traveling down a highway.

"I'm up near the door," she said.

I reached in front of me. My hand clanked against titanium. How was I going to get there if I couldn't see?

I switched to infrared. My world changed from darkness to a cool blue. We were traveling at night, and a quick temperature reading showed it was in the forties, which would have been a heat wave on Mars. Like ghosts, the praying mantis shapes of robots—not quite as blue—emerged from the blue of our surroundings. Even though the truck had been traveling for the almost hour that Ashley and I had spent with Nate and Cannon, the robots had not quite cooled down to the temperature of the rest of the inside of the trailer.

"Ashley, I'm on infrared. Wave an arm!"

Her robot did, and I spotted the arm clearly.

"Give me a minute." I lifted the robot in front of me and held it high above my head. Rolling forward to where it had been standing, I spun and set it down where my robot had just stood. I repeated this several more times until my robot finally stood beside Ashley's robot.

"Hello," I said, bowing gravely. My robot head clanked against the door. The back end of my robot, where the battery was a counterweight, bumped into a robot behind me. The clattering seemed deafening, even with the highway noises as a backdrop. "Oops."

Ashley giggled. Even with all my experience with virtual reality, it was still weird to think that our bodies were actually in blindfolds and headsets in the Arizona desert, while our robots were really only a couple of feet apart. Yet our brain waves sent signals to a computer, which converted them to a digital code and fired them to a satellite that bounced the signals to the receivers on the computers of these robots. Then the robots listened and spoke, and those sound waves were converted into signals bounced back up to the satellite and back down to our bodies, where our brains interpreted them. And all of this back and forth happened at the speed of light—186,000 miles per second—so that our brains responded instantly, as if we were really not controlling our robots but talking person to person.

"Hello," she said. "Since it's hardly been an hour since Dr. Jordan put all of them to sleep, I'll bet we have plenty of time. Which is good. We've got a lot to talk about. I mean, it's been a long time since we last had a chance to speak without someone else listening."

"Since a Federation ship picked us up from the *Moon Racer* near the moon," I said. About a quarter million miles ago.

Ashley and I and my dad had been arrested just outside the orbit of the Moon, put into separate rooms on the ship, taken to Earth, and left alone in separate cells. When we'd escaped, it had been with Nate. He'd been the only one with us until the general showed up to take all of us to a helicopter that allowed us to search for the Institute where Ashley had spent a lot of her childhood.

"Well . . . ," Ashley began.

"Well, what?" It was difficult enough to read her mind when we faced each other person to person. With robots, it was worse. They weren't capable of facial movements, and with only infrared to guide my vision, it would have been impossible to see her expression clearly anyway.

"Well, what's the deal with all the secret stuff that drove the general crazy?"

"Thanks for backing me," I said. I explained my E-mail and that it seemed safer not to trust the general until we knew for sure he wasn't part of the Terratakers.

"All right," she continued. "I understand why you won't trust the general. Yet. What about cutting off the nutrients of the kids in the jelly cylinders? Aren't they suffering enough?"

"Let me ask you something first. Was Stronsky part of the Institute when you were there?"

"Part of it? When we were young, it was fun. Then a few years ago Stronksy showed up and training got serious. He ruled it like a boot camp."

"What about Dr. Jordan?"

"He showed up once in a while to watch our progress," Ashley said. "That was it."

"Which makes sense if he had other pods of robot kids to monitor."

Ashley said nothing. The wind noise and tire-humming noise seemed to grow louder.

"What did I say wrong?" I asked, sensing even in our robot bodies that she was drawing away from me.

"Listen to what you said. Pods of robot kids. Like we're not really human. We are freaks. Not only that, we are freaks created to kill other humans," she said bitterly.

"Not freaks. Not by your choice." The only hope I could give her was something I had suggested to Nate just before going out to the helicopter to send my E-mail to Rawling McTigre. "Besides, no one will be killed once Nate and Cannon get to the right people to delay the meeting of the Federation governors. We all agreed that has to be Jordan's target."

"Bad news there," she said after a pause. "While you were in the helicopter, Cannon made a call to the Supreme Governor to warn him about the soldier robots. The Supreme Governor told Cannon there was no way he could cancel or postpone the Summit of Governors. He says too many people are waiting for an excuse to say the Federation has no power. He says this is the most important Summit in Federation history. They need a renewed commitment to the Mars Project and to world peace. If people—and the rest of the world's governors—found out that robots spawned by the Mars Project were the threat behind a cancellation of the Summit, the Federation might not survive. And the Terratakers would win in the easiest way possible."

I could hardly believe what my robot audio input relayed

to my brain. "So it will be better for the world to learn about us after all the governors are killed?"

"The Supreme Governor told the general there was only one option. That the robots be stopped before the world learns about them. Which is why you and I are here. To find out exactly where these robots are headed."

"But my dad . . . he said we have to expose the robots to the world media and then they'll have to release him from prison."

"Tyce . . ."

By her tone, I knew I wasn't going to like whatever she had to tell me.

"Tyce."

"Yes?"

"That's the other thing I learned in that call. Your dad is gone from prison."

"Gone! How? Where?"

"The Supreme Governor didn't say. He just kept repeating that we had to stop Dr. Jordan and keep the world from knowing about the robots."

Dad. Gone. Was he alive? Had someone taken him?

I was glad to be controlling this robot body. Unlike mine, its arms and fingers wouldn't shake from fear.

"Don't worry," Ashley said. "Cannon and Nate came up with a solution while you were in the helicopter. They say there has to be a transmitter somewhere nearby that beams all our brain waves by computer code to a satellite. While we're gone, Nate's going to look for it. They figure all they have to do is scramble or stop the transmission, and then all these robots here will be unable to respond to Dr. Jordan's commands."

"What about the death chip?" I asked. "If the robots don't listen, he'll activate it. It would be great if once the transmitter was down, the death chips couldn't be activated, but didn't Joey tell us it's on some highly secret cellphone frequency?"

"True. But Cannon and Nate believe that Dr. Jordan will first think if the robots don't respond that it's a computer malfunction. They believe that Dr. Jordan will first try to fix the problem. After all . . ."

Her voice became sadly bitter. "After all, to Dr. Jordan, we're perfect machines and worth a lot of money. That means we're valuable to him. And he wouldn't want to throw us away that quickly."

"But what if Dr. Jordan doesn't realize it's a malfunction? Or what if he gets mad when the robots don't listen to him? What if he hits the death chip button?"

"Better that the people in the Institute die than 200 world leaders. Better that the kids die than a new world war that might happen if the Summit is wrecked." It sounded like Ashley was crying, even though robots can't make tears. "Those were the general's words. Not mine. See? Even to someone who is supposed to be on our side, we're freaks. Disposable machines."

I wanted to be able to comfort her. I searched for words to tell her that she and the other kids were more than just machines. Or freaks. But I couldn't find them. Because deep down—although I had never wanted to admit it to myself—I wondered if she was right.

Freaks. Experiments.

It was true. That's exactly what we were. Ashley, the other kids at the Institute—and me. I'd lived my whole life as a freak because of an experiment gone wrong. I'd never be able to walk like other people could, because Cannon had pushed for funds for a science experiment that would make me a cripple for life. He, Dr. Jordan, and others had used me, just like they'd used the kids in the jelly tubes. Like I was a lab rat. Or a monkey.

It wasn't fair. And I'd have to deal with the unfairness the rest of my life.

I had to wonder, where was God when all this happened? I mean, I had learned to trust him over the last year, and he'd always come through. Even when it seemed we'd die from the oxygen crisis, or that we'd be blown up with the mysterious black boxes. And he'd kept me from despairing when I was locked in the storage room when Jordan and his forces took over the Mars Dome.

But now the crisis was about *me*—personally. And it bothered me like never before because I didn't seem to have any answers.

I wanted to punch a titanium hand against the door of the trailer beside me.

Instead, I forced my mind on what we needed to do next.

"Ashley," I said, "let's see if we can figure out where the truck is."

"From here?"

"From here. We don't have anything else to do."

At least, I thought, until the truck stopped. And then I had no idea what to do after that.

CHAPTER 14

I began to scan beyond my immediate surroundings with my infrared, hoping for anything unusual that might give a hint of the truck's location and destination.

The concept of seeing with infrared isn't much different than seeing with light waves. With light waves bringing your brain information, if you were outside on a hill, you could get on your knees and stare at the grass at your feet. Your focus range would be a matter of inches. Once you stood, you could change your focus and look a couple of feet away at a butterfly on a flower. Then a couple hundred feet away at a cow in the field. Or a couple of miles across the valley. Or upward at the clouds. Or past the horizon. Your eyes can see from inches away to infinity. Cool, if you think about it.

Same with infrared on that same hillside. You could see the grass by its contrasting temperature with the ground. The butterfly on the flower would be outlined by its temperature, even if it varied from the air temperature by a tenth of a degree. Same with the cow. And the clouds.

Because there are these similarities, the only difficult part is practice. But after spending enough time in infrared vision, your brain learns to look for patterns, the same way it does with light-based vision.

The biggest difference is what you can and cannot see inside a room. After all, when you rely on light, the walls block you from seeing the light waves on the other side.

Not with infrared. Unless the walls are totally insulated, you can still see outlines of things on the other side that are producing more heat than the walls or sucking more cold.

As I scanned, I first looked downward. The exhaust pipe of the truck glowed bright red beneath the cool blue of the trailer floor. The tires directly beneath us, heated by contact with the road, were a blur of orange against the dark, dark blue of the road. At the front, I could make out one human-shaped figure in warm orange on the other side of the trailer wall. By his shape, I guessed him to be Stronsky; Dr. Jordan was too important to stay with the robots.

Looking beyond the sides of the trailer didn't show me much. The night air was a darker blue than the trees, which had soaked up heat during the day. The leaves of the trees seemed transparent, almost as if I were seeing a color negative in the light.

Other than that, nothing struck me as unusual.

I wasn't disappointed. I hadn't expected to see much, and I knew even if somehow I could pinpoint the truck's location within a couple of miles, it wouldn't help Nate or Cannon. They had said unless we knew exactly where it was, they wouldn't be able to set up a roadblock.

I fully expected to have to wait until the truck stopped.

Still, I hated wasting time. Even if I was hoping for something else to happen right away. After all, the intravenous tubes had been pinched and . . .

"Tyce?" Ashley's voice was soft in my robot audio system.

"Yes, Ashley?"

"Do you think it's easier to believe in God when things are good in your life? Or when it's bad?"

"What do you mean?"

"Well," she murmured, "I remember all the hours and hours you and I spent at the telescope under the Mars Dome. I loved looking out at the universe. It was even fun doing homework with you. . . . I guess that when you don't have any major problems and your world is so peaceful, it's easy to believe God is like a father who loves you."

"Agreed," I said. Ashley and I often spent time talking together about God. Both of us had learned a lot about him over the past year. Ashley had had a lot of discussions with my dad on the Habitat Lander as they took the six-month journey to Mars. And I'd begun to believe in God after the series of crises on Mars forced me to think about life and death. Since then, I'd come a long way. Now I talked to him a lot. About the big things and the little things. And I'd learned to trust him with my life, even when there were things I didn't understand. Things that made no sense. Like what was happening to the kids in the jelly tubes. Or what had happened to make me a cripple.

On Mars it had seemed natural for Ashley and me to talk about God. Especially with all of the beauty of the universe so easy to see and with so much time on Mars to look. Our thoughts wandered to big questions—like how the universe was made, why was it made, and what that meant for a human living in it.

"But," she continued, "it's times like now, when I feel lost and scared and unsure about what's going to happen, that I wonder if God is really there and if he really does love me. I mean, I know that he does in my head, but I just don't *feel* it in my heart."

I thought about it, knowing that she had been taken away from her parents. All she had of her life before the Institute was the pair of silver earrings in the shape of a cross.

"I think," I said, "it's like when I'm with my parents. When I know they are nearby, I don't have much to worry about. And sometimes I don't even think about their presence. I know they'll take care of me. But if I get taken away, to someplace strange, like Earth—" I grinned—"then they feel very far away. Because we don't feel as close, it makes me miss them more. . . . So in a way, the times you're lonely and afraid are the times that remind you how much you need God. . . . Make sense?" I asked.

"Makes sense," she whispered.

"If it helps," I said, "right now I feel lost and scared and unsure about what's going to happen next. But I'm glad I'm with you. And that God's watching over us too."

"Me too," she said. "I mean, glad to be with you. Not glad to be with myself."

She giggled, then stopped instantly as a voice spoke from a robot somewhere in the middle of the trailer.

"Hey," the voice said, "is it morning? What's happening? Where am I?"

CHAPTER 15

"Hello," I said, directing my robot voice beyond Ashley's robot. "To answer your questions, it's not morning. You're still in the truck. And we're moving somewhere down a highway."

"Not morning!" This came from another robot at the opposite end of the truck. "Why are we awake?"

Other voices began to join in, and it was difficult to hear what anyone was saying. Then robot arms began to stretch, and robot bodies clanked against each other. Video lenses turned in all directions.

Remember, I was seeing this all through infrared. Robots in a lighter blue against a darker blue background. The movement of the skinny stems of the robots and the extended arms and the turning heads looked like a closet full of skeletons coming to life.

"Hello! Hello!" I shouted to get everyone's attention.

That brought relative silence. The wind noise was still loud, and I had to shout to be heard above it.

"Here's what's happened," I said, happy that my guess had been correct. When I wondered about the sleeping drugs that Dr. Jordan used to put the kids to sleep, I realized that he might not want to wake them up at the same time every day. If he administered one big shot when he wanted them to sleep, he'd either have to let it wear off or give them another drug to wake them. It seemed to me it might be simpler if the drugs were put into their bodies on a steady drip that could be shut off automatically on a preset timer in the computer, or manually shut off by instructions to the computer from Dr. Jordan. I began to explain all of this. "Back at the jelly cylinders, your intravenous tubes have been pinched off and—"

"Pinched off! That's the only food we get! We'll starve!"

I could not tell which robot had spoken. "No. There's someone back there to unpinch the tubes. We—"

"Someone's back there? Who? Does Dr. Jordan know?" This from another robot.

"He doesn't know," I said patiently. "That's the whole point of this. So we can talk while he's not watching or listening."

And so that we could talk here through our robot bodies, instead of back at the Institute with the general listening.

"If Dr. Jordan finds out, he'll activate the death chip!"

"We won't let him find out," I answered. "This is our only chance to stop him and—"

"Stop him? Are you crazy? We can't stop him!"

Those words hung in the air. Until someone else asked another question. "Who are you anyway?"

"He's my friend," Ashley said.

"Well, who are you?"

"Ashley, speaking through Number 23."

Immediately buzzing filled the inside of the trailer as all the robots began to speak at once. It only ended when another robot shouted for silence.

"Let me through," the robot insisted when the other voices quieted. "I'll speak for all of us."

There was more clanking and rolling as the robots moved with difficulty. Through the bluish haze, I saw one robot push forward until it reached Ashley's and mine.

"Ashley," the robot said. The voice was not friendly. "This is Kurt speaking. I see you're back."

"Kurt!" Ashley responded. She sounded friendly. A little *too* friendly for my liking. "I missed you! But I couldn't say anything before when Stronsky was around. Let me tell you though, if robots could hug, I'd hug you."

Missed him? Hug? Now I definitely didn't like the friend-liness in her voice.

"I wouldn't let you hug me," Kurt retorted through his robot. "Not after what you did. Did you get them to fake your death after you escaped?"

"Me?"

"Don't play dumb. What did you two do now—kill Michael and Joey to take their places?"

"What!"

"I guess two more deaths wouldn't matter to you." Kurt sounded bitter. "After all, because of you, half of us got to learn from the other half how the death chips work. And because of you, a bunch of new kids had to replace that first half."

"Half? Killed? Death chips?"

"The half who had agreed with you to try to escape. Stronsky told us what you did. Gave him their names so you could be set free and leave the rest of us behind. But he told us you'd been killed too, which made us all very happy."

"What!" Ashley sounded like she was in shock. "That's not true. I had no choice. Dr. Jordan took me away."

"More like he brought you back to spy on us again," Kurt threw back.

"No! Dr. Jordan took me to the Mars Dome. He—"

"Mars," Kurt interrupted. I heard a sneer in his voice. *"Right.* Most of Earth knows the *truth* about the Mars Dome."

Much as I wanted to punch this robot with my own titanium fists, I simply asked, "Which is?"

"There's no Mars Dome. It's all a fake. Every time the Federation wants to keep people happy about sucking the world's resources, they bring out new media stuff showing progress on Mars. But we all know it's some computer-generated images that any Hollywood producer could put together."

"I see," I said.

"You do?" Again, I sensed the sneer that could not be hidden through a robot's speakers. "And who exactly are you? I mean, being Ashley's friend isn't a good thing."

"Me? I was the first kid born on Mars."

Kurt laughed, and other robot laughter grew behind him.

Although I knew better—that one robot punching another would not prove much—emotion won. I raised my fist.

Ashley stepped between us. "Listen," she insisted, "there will be time to sort all of this out later. And when we're done, you'll see that Tyce and I are telling the truth. For now, though, we have to work together."

"Why?" Kurt asked loudly. "Even if we could trust you, why should we risk our lives and work against Dr. Jordan and Stronsky? You heard what he said today about our parents."

"Whenever this truck gets to where it is going," I said, "they are going to use us as an army."

"We know that." The sneer again. "It's just some more training. In some sort of virtual-reality war game."

"Not a game," I said. "You'll be shooting real people. The governors of every country of the world. Dr. Jordan wants us to destroy their Summit meeting and start a new world war."

"Hah, hah, hah," Kurt said. "You and Ashley make quite a pair. First you've been to Mars, and now we're going to start a world war."

"Maybe we should listen to them," a voice in the back said.

"Really," Kurt said sarcastically. "So Dr. Jordan can get a new list of the rebels among us? So he'll activate a bunch more death chips? So our parents will be killed?"

I jumped in because I didn't want to allow anyone to answer. "We can prove we're telling the truth," I said. In the blue haze, robot heads swiveled my way. "Why don't a few of you jump out of robot control and go back?"

"Back?" came a voice. This one sounded afraid. "I'd rather be asleep than wake up back in the jelly cylinder. I can't see or hear, and my body feels so trapped."

"What's your answer to *that?*" Kurt said.

"Simple. Those of you who go back just call out for help. General Cannon and a guy named Nate will help you take off the wax over your eyes and ears so you can see and hear. Then you'll see Michael and Joey. You'll know they're alive. And the general and Nate will tell you why we need to stop Dr. Jordan."

"Fine then," Kurt said. "We'll do that." He spoke to everyone else. "I need three volunteers."

He got them.

It took less than a minute for all three to return to controlling their robots.

"Kurt," the first one said, "these two are lying to us."

CHAPTER 16

"Lying?" I raised my robot arms in protest. "Impossible."

"No one came," the first kid said. "I screamed for help. No one came. It was horrible, feeling my body stuck there. Like a spider had me all wrapped up. I was blind and deaf. Finally I came back here. At least when I control my robot, my brain doesn't feel like it's stuck in a black box."

The other robot voices began to babble again.

"Silence!" Kurt shouted.

As the truck roared down the highway, the voices died down.

"Do you other two agree?"

They both said yes. No one had helped them.

"And that from three of us who have no reason to lie," Kurt put in. "Because if there was a chance to be rescued, we would take it. Three of us against two of them. We know Ashley already turned traitor against us. And a friend of hers is probably an enemy of ours."

I could hardly believe this. We were their only hope, and yet there was nothing Ashley and I could do to get them to believe us. It was like believing in God. As my mom used to say, she couldn't force me to believe in God. I had to choose to believe in him on my own. And that's exactly what these kids had to do. Choose to believe in us on their own.

"I would say," Kurt continued, "that it's obvious what we should do."

"No," Ashley protested. "Listen to me. I was sent to Mars. I was supposed to test a space torpedo called the Hammerhead. But it was intended to kill millions of people. So instead I crashed it into one of the moons of Mars. Then Tyce came back with me to help find you guys. Dr. Jordan, who was in a prison on the ship, took over the computer and escaped in a pod. He had programmed the spaceship to crash into the sun, but we . . ." Her voice trailed off as she realized how crazy it must sound to the other kids.

"Hah, hah, hah," Kurt answered. "This isn't story time, you know. And we're not stupid." Then he spoke to the other robots. "You know what Stronsky promised when we began training in these war games. Once we prove ourselves to Dr. Jordan, he's going to let us show the entire world what we can do. Then people will know that armies like ours can protect them. We'll be heroes."

Some of the kids cheered at this.

Kurt paused. "Not only will we be heroes, we'll still be alive. Which definitely won't happen if we follow these two against Dr. Jordan."

"You're wrong," I said. I raised my voice to the others. "The only way you can stay alive is by defeating Dr. Jordan."

Voices began to chatter again.

"Everyone!" Kurt shouted. "Listen!"

They listened.

"You know they're lying to us," he said. "I say we tear their bot-packs off so they can't try anything here. In the morning Dr. Jordan can activate their death chips. That will catch up with them, no matter how far they run in their real bodies."

Our death chips?

Ashley spoke my thoughts. "Kurt, I wasn't around when you were put in the jelly cylinders. The death chips don't scare me."

Kurt laughed. "You weren't around because you turned traitor. But you also missed hearing everything they told us about the death chips, didn't you?"

Ashley's silence told him enough.

"See," he taunted, "the same satellite that beams our signals to the robots will also beam an activation signal anytime Stronsky or Jordan want. Just like a global positioning unit, the signal will track you down. Then *poof!* You're dead."

"Not me," Ashley said, with a little less certainty than before.

"Of course, you. We found out they didn't implant the death chips when they put us in the jelly cylinders. No, they did it when they operated on us for the spinal plugs. All those years we never knew that little bomb was waiting inside us. Not until we watched half of us die. The half that you betrayed.

"Yes, Ashley. We saw Stronsky push the button, and they died—in front of us. Just slowly fell and then stopped moving. In the morning, the same will happen to you. Justice will be served."

"Please," I said intensely. "Listen to Ashley. She's telling you the truth. She didn't betray any of you."

"Then how did Stronsky know the ones who were planning to try to escape?"

I had no answer for that. Neither did Ashley. But we knew the story couldn't be true.

"Then consider yourselves guilty," Kurt insisted. "OK, everyone. Time to vote. Here's the plan of action. We tear the bot-packs off their robot bodies and disable them. In the morning, we report this to Dr. Jordan and let him activate the death chip. How many yes votes?"

In the hazy blue, there was no movement behind him. Not at first. Then one hand went up. And another two. Another three.

It didn't take a genius to figure out where this was headed. If we were still connected when the bot-packs were torn off our bodies, it could blow our own brain circuits. Sudden disconnection was far worse than any shock.

"Ashley," I said urgently, "we'd better go."

Without waiting for her to say anything, I shouted *Stop!* in my mind to release myself from robot control.

And fell into darkness.

CHAPTER 17

Back in the jelly cylinder room, I shouted as I tore at my blindfold and headset. "Ashley! Ashley!"

Finally clear of my blindfold, I saw her sitting against the wall, motionless.

Nate and Cannon were gone. So were Michael and Joey.

"Ashley!" I began to wheel toward her. "Ashley!"

I knew she couldn't hear me, not with her ears covered, but that didn't stop me from shouting again. "Ashley!"

Then I saw her hands move, and I let out a deep sigh of relief.

As I reached her, she was taking off her own blindfold. She blinked her eyes a couple of times in order to focus on this room. And then she smiled.

"Ashley."

"I'm back," she said. "Where are the others?"

"Not sure. But it explains why the three kids who returned didn't get any help." I pointed at the jelly cylinders where the intravenous tubes were pinched and tied with pieces of shoelace. "We've got to untie those tubes and get them all back to sleep again. And then figure something out in the remaining hours until Dr. Jordan wakes them up."

The other four returned about 10 minutes later, with Michael and Joey trailing the big men in front of them.

"You're back," Cannon said. "I thought we agreed you were going to stay with all the other robots and try to find out what was planned next."

Ashley quickly filled them in.

"Let me get this straight," he said when she finished. "The truck is going to arrive at its destination, and you won't be able to get back into your robots because they were disconnected."

"Yes, sir," I answered for her. "I doubt we put them to sleep fast enough to prevent them from disconnecting the robot computers."

"And as soon as Dr. Jordan wakes them up and talks to them, he'll learn about you two. And he'll . . ." I could tell the general's mind was racing ahead.

"Yes, sir. If the death chip works like he says, Ashley's chip will be activated."

"Michael." The general turned to him. "Was everything Kurt told these two correct? Half of your group?"

"Right in front of us," Michael said, shivering. "Stronsky showed us his little remote. He let us watch him push the button. They all slowly fell down. And then some of the aides dragged them away. The next morning a bunch of younger kids were brought in to replace them. In the afternoon they put us all in the jelly cylinders."

The general frowned. He turned his gaze back to me. "Why only Ashley's death chip? Why not yours?"

Mine?

"Sir, I wasn't part of this group of kids. My operation took place on Mars."

"What makes you assume Dr. Jordan doesn't have a death chip implanted in you too?"

"I . . . I . . ." I couldn't come up with an answer. Horror filled me as I understood. If the death chip were part of the operation, why wouldn't it have been done to me too?

When the truck arrived at its destination, and as soon as Dr. Jordan woke up the robots and found out that Ashley and I had survived, he would press a little button and send a signal that would stop our hearts.

Cannon closed his eyes, then opened them again. He spoke very quietly. "This changes things, doesn't it?"

CHAPTER 18

I was back in the helicopter again at my unfolded comp-board, with my system just booted. Yes, we were running out of time, and Ashley and I should have been doing something else. But what? Cannon, Nate, Joey, Michael, Ashley, and I had spent the last 45 minutes trying to come up with a solution.

And we couldn't decide on anything.

I desperately wanted some good news.

Like the fact that Rawling had read my E-mail and been able to reply.

My comp-board had finally loaded and connected to the Internet. I stared glumly at my computer screen as I accessed Cannon's E-mail account.

Then I smiled as I read the first and only message. With all that had gone wrong, I at least knew now that I could trust Cannon.

From: "Rawling McTigre" <mctigrer@marsdome.ss>
To: "General Jeb McNamee"
<mcnameej@combatforce.gov>
Sent: 03.31.2040, 12:05 A.M.
Subject: Re: Please read this right away!

Tyce, when you banged your robot head during that expedition, I said it was as hard as your own stubborn skull and that you were so used to banging it against things that you no longer needed any pills for a headache.

Yes, it's me. And I'm so relieved to hear from you. The real you.

Yes, I had been getting responses to the E-mails I'd been sending you, but they were strange responses and I was beginning to wonder if it really was you. In fact, during the last week I had a trusted computer programmer go through the mainframe, and he found the secret programming that allowed someone in the dome to intercept all the messages. It's a long story—one that I want to tell you when you get back—but right now I'm playing cat and mouse, sending real E-mails with one program and fake E-mails with the other program. I'm hoping to find out who here on Mars is secretly logging on to the mainframe.

In short, you can trust this message. I wish I could do more than this though. Your E-mail brought up too many disturbing questions, and I'm 50 million miles away.

By the urgency of your message, I hope and expect you will check your E-mail soon. I've dropped everything here and am waiting in front of my computer screen for your reply to this. (I've printed out your Moon Racer diary and will read it as I wait so that I'll be as up-to-date as possible.)

I know there is a time lag, but as soon as I get your next E-mail, I'll send you one back. It will be the closest thing we can have to a live conversation.

And Tyce? I'll be praying too.

Your friend, Rawling

P.S. I don't want to say anything to your mother until I know as much as possible. I'm worried enough. She'll go through the roof of the dome unless I can answer all her questions.

It gave me strength to know that Rawling was waiting. And praying. So I began to type.

From: "General Jeb McNamee"
<mcnameej@combatforce.gov>
To: "Rawling McTigre" <mctigrer@marsdome.ss>
Sent: 03.31.2040, 12:26 A.M.
Subject: GOT IT

Rawling! Thanks! Just sending this to let you know I've read your E-mail. During the lag for this to reach you and your next message to reach me, I'll put together a longer one with more details and send it ASAP.

Your friend, Tyce

I hit send. Then I immediately began to explain all that I could in a longer E-mail. I knew I had about 20 minutes before I heard back from Rawling.

There wasn't much good news. Actually, there wasn't *any* good news. Starting with the fact that my dad had disappeared from prison, and that now, even if we stopped Dr. Jordan, I wouldn't know how to find Dad.

Here, Cannon and Nate had gone searching for the transmitter with Michael and Joey. That's why they were gone when the three kids tried to verify Ashley's story. The bad news was that they hadn't been able to find the transmitter in the darkness.

Nate had suggested that since Ashley and I could no

longer secretly work among the robot soldiers, we should just unplug all the kids from their jelly cylinders. That way none of the robots would be operational, and Dr. Jordan wouldn't hear about Ashley and me from any of the other kids.

Cannon then told us he was about to make the most difficult decision he'd ever made as a general. That he couldn't do that, even if it would save our lives. Then he explained why.

Since they couldn't find the transmitter here on the mountain, he would have to call in for Combat Force surveillance to use three of their satellites to triangulate the signals from here to Dr. Jordan's receiving satellite. Because this required three Combat Force satellites, it would take hours for all of them to be in the required positions. Then, once they were in position, we'd need exactly 20 minutes to triangulate the location.

When I asked why Dr. Jordan's satellite was so important, Cannon said there were thousands of satellites in orbit. They'd have to find it first. Once they did, they could pull it in and find out where it had been sending and receiving other signals, because that would allow the Combat Force to find all the other pods of kids.

Timing was crucial then. I pointed out that Dr. Jordan might move the army so quickly that the robot soldiers would be in position to kill immediately. Cannon's solution was to have someone call him at the first sign of trouble, at which he would unplug the kids here and shut down their robot control. That was not good. Being shocked into disconnection was bad enough. But to be unplugged without warning . . .

It meant that in worst-case scenario some of the kids would die, and most of them would suffer brain damage.

The time to unplug them was *before* they went into control mode. Once their brains were actively engaged with the robot computer, any short circuit or disconnection caused brutal damage.

Just as I finished putting all of this into my E-mail, my computer chirped, telling me I had mail. I held off on sending my message and opened and scanned what Rawling had sent me.

From: "Rawling McTigre" <mctigrer@marsdome.ss>
To: "General Jeb McNamee"
<mcnameej@combatforce.gov>
Sent: 03.31.2040, 12:55 A.M.
Subject: WAITING AT MY COMPUTER

All right, Tyce, send me what you have. Hopefully I won't have many questions, and hopefully I can answer any questions you have for me.

Rawling

Questions for him? Sure. Like how Ashley and I might stop Dr. Jordan from activating our death chips. Or how Cannon might stop Jordan after he had killed us by activating our death chips. I didn't word it exactly like that, but I hoped I got the message across. I just finished my E-mail by asking Rawling to offer any suggestions, and most of all, to continue to pray for us. I also sent a hug through him to my mom. I knew she'd be terribly worried once she found out about all of this.

I sent this message and began my wait again. As the minutes ticked by with incredible slowness, I decided to write another E-mail. This one to my mother. To tell her how much I loved her and how much she meant to me. Even more, how glad I was that she had talked to me a lot about God as I was growing up—even when I didn't want to hear about him. And that she'd given me the freedom to decide for myself what I believed, instead of trying to force me to believe what she did. As a result, I'd realized that everything she'd said about God was true. And I'd come to share her Christian faith.

I held off on sending the E-mail, though, because I knew it would make her too sad.

Somewhere inside me, I still had a little hope. Maybe Rawling would think of something we had missed.

His next message arrived exactly 20 minutes later.

From: "Rawling McTigre" <mctigrer@marsdome.ss>
To: "General Jeb McNamee"
<mcnameej@combatforce.gov>
Sent: 03.31.2040, 1:15 A.M.
Subject: Re: The whole story

Tyce, I've received your E-mail. Hang tight on your end while I think things through.

Rawling

I hung tight. And exactly one hour later, his next E-mail arrived. It showed that, yes, Rawling *had* thought things through.

I called for Grunt, the helicopter pilot, to help me back down to the ground and into my wheelchair.

And I rolled as fast as I could back toward the jelly cylinders.

CHAPTER 19

"Ugly and weird. We drove 36 hours to deliver these?"

We were glad for that 36 hours. Without that one extra day of travel, Ashley and I would probably be so sleep-deprived we'd never have a chance to succeed.

After getting that E-mail from Rawling, it had been a lot easier to return from the helicopter to the general. Cannon could be trusted. So I'd told him everything.

We'd come up with a plan.

Then we'd slept, since Cannon insisted rested soldiers were effective soldiers.

After waking, almost at noon the next day, all of us had waited in suspense as Cannon had found some trusted people in the military to begin a search for the moving truck. It was a next-to-impossible chance to find it but worth trying, because then we could stop the robot soldiers with no risk.

Instead, the hours had dragged on while we got everything ready that we could. Then Cannon had insisted that Ashley and I sleep again. He'd woken us up at midnight, and she and I had been controlling the robot bodies in the trailer ever since.

Just waiting for the truck to stop.

Which was now.

The truck driver had opened the door to the trailer. He spoke to his assistant, who stood beside him. They looked similar. Shaved heads, skinny, in leather jackets and blue jeans. Both puffed on cigarettes as they surveyed all the robots. Including the new ones that Ashley and I now controlled.

"No wonder that muscle freak left us alone to do this," his helper agreed. They stood on a warehouse dock. Nothing in the background gave any clues as to where we had stopped after hours in the trailer among the motionless robots. "These are really, really ugly. Really, really weird. Like a bunch of stick insects I seen on the Nature Channel accidentally one night when I was looking for music videos. What do you call them? Paving mantras?"

The first part of our plan had been the simplest. Since robots 17 and 23 had disconnected computers, Cannon and Nate had helped two other kids out of jelly cylinders and Ashley and I had replaced them. I was now Number 9, and Ashley was 16. Back in the desert mountains, those kids were now out of their jelly cylinders and happy to be moving around normally.

"Paving Mantras?" the driver said. "I ain't heard of that rock band."

"Not a rock band. That's the name of those stick insects. Paving mantras."

"*Paying* mantras is more like it," the driver said, flicking ashes. "We've never made easier money. Keys were in the truck like the guy on the phone said. Map was waiting. And for a change, New York traffic wasn't bad."

"You've never been up before 10 in the morning," the second guy said. "Of course you wouldn't know what the streets are like this early."

The first man sucked hard on his cigarette and grinned. "Still haven't been up before 10 in the morning."

"Huh?"

"Haven't gone to sleep yet. But as soon as we unload these creepy things, I'm gonna spend a wad of money on a fancy hotel room and sleep and sleep. Driving all night ain't my idea of a good time. I'm gonna get up only to order room service and fill my face. How does that sound?"

"Me," the second guy put in, "I've got a list of horses that can't lose. I'm taking my money and tripling it at the racetracks."

"Yeah, yeah. Got those directions that were under the mat? Remember, the guy said the money would be waiting for us in the storage room where we deliver these."

"I got the directions. You got the keys and passwords to get into this building?"

"Yup. Good thing," the first guy said. He threw his cigarette down. "You know them governors are meeting at some kind of Summit around here. I don't think you could get into any of these buildings without a password for the security pads."

"Yeah. That voice on the phone must be well connected."

"He's got money. You got money, you got connections."

It was the second guy's turn to grin. "I guess then you and me have now got connections."

One by one they began to lift out the robots in front of Ashley and me. I noticed that 17 and 23 had loose wires dangling where the bot-packs had been ripped away. Neither the driver nor his assistant noticed, however. They treated those two robots like the others. Once on the dock they rolled each one out of sight. I couldn't see where they went, but they weren't gone long between each robot, and Ashley and I didn't dare speak to each other.

The trailer was empty of robots before they reached ours.

"What do you think these things do?" the second guy asked, picking up the robot that Ashley controlled.

The first guy shrugged. "Got to be for some kind of science-fiction movie. You know, just another story where something attacks someone in New York City."

"Yeah, yeah. Someone in movies has the kind of money to call us up and tell us where to find this truck. I mean, all of it was right there like he promised."

The first guy leaned forward to pick up my robot. His face was so close to my video lens that I could see his blackheads oozing out of his pores. Cradling my robot in his arms, he walked onto the dock, into the building, and then pushed the robot forward down the hallway. He reached the storage room as his assistant was stepping out. They squeezed by each other.

Even with all the sleep that the general had insisted we get, the stress of suspense had made me feel a little goofy. At least that's my only explanation for what I did next, without even thinking about it. With my hand low and out of sight, I pinched the assistant's leg as we passed him in the doorway.

"Hey! Why'd you do that?"

"Do what?" the driver said, pushing my robot among the others and turning to face his assistant.

"Don't mess with me, man. Were you trying to take the money out of my pocket?"

"Me?"

"Like who else grabbed me?"

"You saying I grabbed you?"

The door to the storage room slammed shut. Their voices disappeared gradually as they continued to argue.

In the dimness of the storage room, Ashley giggled. "I saw what you did," she said. "I just wish you could have seen the look on the guy's face."

I laughed with her, but neither of us laughed for long.

We knew what was ahead.

CHAPTER 20

I could not guess how much time had passed since all the robots had been unloaded into this large storage room. But each second seemed like a year. Ashley and I didn't talk— we didn't know when one of the robots around us might wake. And we didn't know when Dr. Jordan or Stronsky or both of them would open the storage room door. It was too important now that our identity among the other robots remain a secret.

As we waited, my mind kept going in circles. About the only question that had been answered by the two deliverymen was our approximate location. We were in downtown New York City. And near the Summit meeting. Which meant the targets were definitely the governors of the Federation.

But how did Dr. Jordan intend to get us into the room?

More importantly, when?

The best case would be as late as possible. The brain-wave activity that Ashley and I were sending to these robots was enough transmission for the Combat Force satellites to get the location of Dr. Jordan's receiving satellite. Those three satellites would be in the right positions to triangulate at 7:00 A.M. Arizona time—9:00 A.M. New York time. And it would take 20 minutes for the triangulation. If Dr. Jordan didn't intend to attack until after that, Cannon and Nate would be able to get Dr. Jordan's satellite position, then unplug all the other kids, before they were hooked up through virtual reality, so every robot in this room would be useless. That would leave me and Ashley to face Dr. Jordan and Stronsky as they opened the door.

But if Dr. Jordan's attack was planned before 9:20 . . .

That's what made waiting so difficult. Thinking about the worst-case scenario.

Cannon would wait as long as possible to unplug the kids, hoping for enough time to triangulate. But he was on a direct cell-phone line to someone he'd sent to join the governors. If these robots somehow managed to breach security and reach the Summit meeting, he'd have to pull the plug on each of the kids in the jelly tubes except for me and Ashley. And because they'd be actively connected to the robots through virtual reality, their brains would never be the same.

And Ashley and I would remain in robot control, because if everyone else was unplugged, it was crucial for Ashley and me to continue our brain-wave transmissions for the triangulation efforts.

Worst of all, we'd have to face Dr. Jordan and his death chip activator.

I sure hoped Rawling's theories about all of this were right.

I let all these thoughts circle through my mind until finally, finally, I heard sound.

Of robots waking up around me.

Shortly after that, the storage room door opened.

Dr. Jordan and Stronsky stood framed against the light.

"Good morning, boys and girls," Dr. Jordan said. "Are we all awake and ready for a big day?"

"Last night we had to disconnect the computers to Numbers 17 and 23," Kurt reported. His robot stood in the hallway, alone with Dr. Jordan and Stronsky. Barely 30 seconds after the door opened, Kurt had raised his robot arm to tattle on us.

"Numbers 17 and 23," Stronsky repeated.

I was listening to them because I had amplified my hearing. Trouble was, to get their words, the background noise had to be a lot higher too. I could also hear the scratching of cockroaches in the nearby walls, a sound I'd learned, to my disgust, during my time in the Florida prison. "I'm not surprised. Those two gave me trouble during yesterday's training session."

"Shut up, idiot," Dr. Jordan hissed. "Don't you understand? If this happened last night, that means the kids weren't asleep."

His tone changed as he directed his next words to Kurt's robot. "Isn't that right, Number 19?"

"Yes, sir. It was the weirdest thing. Just like that, I popped awake. So I started robot control, expecting to see you. But we were in the back of the trailer. Everyone else woke up, and Ashley started to tell us—"

"Ashley!" Dr. Jordan interrupted Kurt with fierceness that would have scared a bear protecting her cubs.

"Yes, Ashley. I mean, I know you sent her there to test us to see who would rebel against you. I thought it would be better to make her quiet so that the younger kids wouldn't be tempted to do something stupid. I mean, you asked me to protect them by reporting everything to you."

There was a long pause. "You did send her, didn't you?" Kurt asked, his uncertainty amplified 100 times in my robot hearing.

I could guess what Kurt was suddenly thinking. Because if Dr. Jordan had not sent Ashley, then it meant Ashley had been telling the truth. She wasn't a traitor to the rest of the kids.

"Of course I sent her," Dr. Jordan said after the briefest of pauses.

"That's what I thought, sir." Kurt sounded relieved. If my robot had had teeth, I'd have been grinding them at how badly Kurt was trying to be a teacher's pet. "I have to admit, that Tyce person sounded like the real thing for a second or two. His story about being from Mars fit exactly with what she was telling us."

"Tyce!" Dr. Jordan sucked in a breath. Now I could imagine what he was thinking. That I was supposed to be dead. "Yes, Tyce. So you disconnected their robot computers? Did anything else happen?"

"No, sir. I might have dozed off. Next thing I knew we were all here in this storage room."

"Thank you, Number 19."

"I just thought of something," Kurt added. "You're not going to activate the death chip on them, are you? I mean, if they're secretly working for you . . ."

"Of course not." I wondered if Dr. Jordan simply meant not while Kurt was watching. Because then Kurt would realize that Ashley and I were enemies of Dr. Jordan.

I heard Kurt's robot wheels squeak against the floor as he turned away. Then another squeak. He'd pivoted back to Dr. Jordan.

"You will remember all my help, won't you?" Kurt asked.

"After this is over, you will free me from the cylinder like you promised?"

"Of course," Dr. Jordan said smoothly. "Just remember to do your best in this next mission. We're almost ready to begin."

Kurt rolled back to join us.

Dr. Jordan remained in the hallway. He didn't talk to Stronsky. Probably because he was thinking through what he had just learned from Kurt. Among his lies to Kurt was the one that meant the most to Ashley and me.

The one where he had promised Kurt that he wouldn't activate our death chips.

I knew that was a lie for three reasons. One, since he knew that Ashley and I had taken control of a couple of robots here, he also knew that she and I were back at the Institute, thousands of miles away, where the only way he could stop us quickly was by killing us.

Two, he knew from Kurt that Ashley and I had spent part of last night trying to convince all the other kids to help us. Which meant to him that if Ashley and I were still alive and back at the Institute, we would be doing our best to stop him.

And three, he had already tried to kill us a couple of times by other means.

So I waited, wondering what would happen to the heart in my body back at the Institute. Wondering if blinding pain would take me away from robot control. Wondering if I would die in the next 30 seconds.

CHAPTER 21

I did not die in the next 30 seconds. Or the next minute.

Which meant Rawling had guessed right. The first part of his last E-mail to me had been very simple:

Tyce, I doubt Dr. Jordan would kill the kids in the jelly tubes. He has invested too much time and money in their operations and training. My guess is he wanted to replace some of the older kids with younger ones and ship the older kids somewhere else, so he made it look like he had killed them. It would be easy. Slip some sort of knockout capsule in their food and activate it with everyone watching. Pretend to make them an example and tell everyone that Ashley had betrayed them. I know it will be gambling with your life, but if he really has the power to activate the death chip, you have nothing to lose. I think it's a bluff. There's no such thing as a death chip. Why? Because if Dr. Jordan had really implanted a death chip in you and Ashley, he'd have activated it a long time ago the other times he had tried killing you. I'm sure he is very, very annoyed that he hasn't gotten rid of you yet!

Inside the storage shed, I slowly moved the robot head to look over at the robot that Ashley controlled. She, in turn, had swiveled its head to look at my robot. She nodded slightly. I did the same to her.

We were still alive!

Dr. Jordan stepped into the doorway again to address us. Stronsky was nowhere to be seen.

Now came the difficult part.

Dr. Jordan checked his watch. "In 15 minutes, your targets will be assembled. At that time the computer will arm your lasers. Five minutes after that, you will complete your mission."

He surveyed the robots. "Your task today will be no different than the way you have trained for this mission. Number 19 will lead you. He will throw a smoke bomb immediately upon entering the room. Switch to infrared and destroy the targets. Thus, in 20 minutes, I want all of them dead."

"Dead?" This came from robot 9. "This is a virtual-reality mission, right? To prove we can be great soldiers."

"Yes, yes," Dr. Jordan said in a soothing voice. He glanced at his watch again. "None of you need to worry about a thing."

"But it seems you've gone to a lot of trouble and—"

Dr. Jordan interrupted by pulling a small remote from his pocket and aiming it at Number 9. "Let's see," Dr. Jordan said, staring down at the remote, "I punch in 9 and . . ."

"No!" the kid controlling the robot yelled. "I believe you."

I desperately wanted to tell all the kids it was a bluff. That Rawling had been right. There was no death chip. But if I did that and Dr. Jordan thought he was on the verge of losing control, he himself might use his remote control to shut down the transmission from the satellite. And we still needed time to triangulate. It wouldn't happen without a continuous stream of digital signals bouncing back and forth.

"Let me remind all of you," Dr. Jordan threatened. "If just one of you disobeys or tries to stop this mission, I will activate the death chip in the heart of every single person here." He looked carefully at all of the robots. "There are two of you here who know what I mean."

So he'd guessed that Ashley and I had returned by using different robots!

But he hadn't guessed we knew he was only bluffing about the death chip. So that meant we had a better shot at stopping him from killing the governors at the Summit meeting. But would we be able to get the triangulation signal before Cannon unplugged all the kids in their jelly cylinders? If that happened, it would be just like activating a death chip because some of the kids might die.

"Two of us here know what you mean?" Kurt repeated.

"Oh, shut your whining mouth," Dr. Jordan snapped. "We're down to 17 minutes. Follow me to the street. Stronsky will take over from there."

CHAPTER 22

Twenty-one of us rolled our robots as we followed Stronsky down the sidewalk, with hundreds of passersby barely glancing at us. So this was what the truck driver and his assistant had meant about New York. Nothing was new, and nobody was impressed at anything. We could have been invisible, for all the city's reaction to 21 robots rolling in single file.

I glanced around. A bright sun beamed down from a beautiful blue sky. I was barely used to seeing blue sky as it was—on Mars the sky is butterscotch colored—and I realized I hadn't seen much light at all in the last couple of days. Plus, all my thoughts had been so filled with stress, it just seemed like the world was dark.

I'd forgotten how amazing a blue sky could look.

And, since I'd never been in a big city before, I was also amazed at the buildings and vehicles and the sheer number of people who ignored us as they flowed around the robots.

The noise was nearly overwhelming. Horns, shouting, sirens.

This was New York City!

I wished badly I could just be a tourist. Not a freak controlling a robot because someone had operated on me when I was little.

But I had to worry about time.

We approached a large public square surrounded by grandiose buildings, and on one of them, a large clock plainly showed the time. I checked it against my hidden countdown device.

Twelve minutes past nine. The triangulation had begun 12 minutes ago! The three Federation satellites in three different orbits were tracking the transmission beams that came from the mountaintop in Arizona. As soon as they'd been able to gather enough data, they could fire a laser at Dr. Jordan's satellite and knock it out of orbit. All transmissions to these robots would end.

Twelve minutes past nine.

Eight minutes to go.

And what looked like now only five minutes until we reached the building where the Summit of Governors met.

Was there a way Ashley or I could slow down this procession?

As we neared the largest building five minutes later, I relaxed. Twenty armed Federation soldiers guarded the entrance. They wouldn't let us in without a fight. Surely that would take more than a couple of minutes.

That's all we needed. A delay.

Except as we rolled up the wheelchair ramp to the wide doors of the main entrance, the soldiers stepped aside.

One of them saluted Stronsky.

All of the soldiers were on the side of the Terratakers!

We entered with no delay at all.

Now three minutes and counting . . .

I looked around for Dr. Jordan. That had been the next part of the plan: to take him hostage as we approached the

Summit. That way he'd be prisoner, and we could hold him long enough for the triangulation to finish.

No Dr. Jordan.

Instead, the robots continued to roll down a wide hallway, with a nice carpet that hushed the sound of our wheels.

Where was Dr. Jordan?!

At the end of the long hallway four more Federation soldiers guarded another gleaming door.

We'd get there in less than a minute. But my countdown device showed we needed at least two more minutes for successful triangulation for the satellite to be disabled. Two minutes. Which we desperately needed. If those soldiers ahead let us through as well, one of two things would happen. The robots would kill the governors. Or back in the desert, Cannon would be forced to unplug all the kids in the cylinders while they were still connected, killing or brain-damaging them.

Where was Dr. Jordan?!

All right then, I told myself. *Take Stronksy.*

I sped up the rolling of my wheels and reached him. Grabbing his arm, I spun him toward me.

"What?" he snarled. Few men were bigger than he was, and even fewer carried more muscle bulk. Yet he couldn't shake off my robot's grasp. The machine in my control was five times more powerful than the world's best human soldiers. "Let go!"

"No. Stop all these robots."

"Have you lost your mind!" he exclaimed. "You want Dr. Jordan activating all the death chips?"

"We both know there are no death chips. Now give the order to stop!" I put my other hand around his throat and applied pressure. "You know the strength these robots have, Stronsky. Your neck will be skinnier than a pencil when I finish squeezing."

"Tyce, I wondered when you would try your usual cheeseball heroics. Only this time it won't work." Dr. Jordan's voice came from a miniature walkie-talkie on a string around Stronsky's massive neck. "Surprised to hear from me? Did you really think I wouldn't find a way to monitor this?"

"Stop the kids," I said. I squeezed harder and Stronsky grunted. "Or I activate Stronsky's death chip the old-fashioned way."

"I highly doubt that, Tyce. You haven't got the guts to kill him. Besides, even if you did, you wouldn't be able to stop the robots. They don't trust you, and you don't have enough time to explain." Dr. Jordan stopped, then addressed Stronsky. "Stronsky, are you near the Summit doors?"

"Ten yards," he grunted.

"Good. Proceed as planned."

Even though I had Stronsky by the neck, he waved all the robots forward.

CHAPTER 23

"Stop!" I had to delay them just one more minute.

"Stop?" The squealing protest came from, of course, Kurt, who was running Number 19. "Are you trying to get all of us killed?"

"No, I—"

The robots kept rolling forward.

"Really," Ashley pleaded. "Stop! You don't have to kill anyone!"

None of the robots slowed down.

This was too crazy. We'd actually found a way to stop Dr. Jordan and rescue the kids from the jelly cylinders, but they wouldn't listen. They didn't believe us. And because of it, they were less than a minute away from being unplugged from their robots. It seemed like there was nothing we could do to save them.

The soldiers ahead stepped aside. One of them began to open the door. They too were Terratakers who had infiltrated the Federation army!

A deep voice reached us. I recognized it. It belonged to the old man I'd met in prison. The man my father had been holding at knifepoint in the cell. The man I'd found out later was the Supreme Governor, the man with the most political power in the world. From where I was in the hallway, I could see his distinguished features at a podium as he spoke into a microphone.

No! I wanted to shout in frustration. In 30 more seconds, the triangulation would be complete, the transmitting satellite disabled. But Kurt was almost through the doorway, ready to toss the smoke bomb that would lead to the deaths of all these governors. We wouldn't get those seconds!

"Aaaaagh!"

In my panic, I'd forgotten I was still clutching Stronsky by the neck. As my frustration and panic grew, I'd accidentally begun to squeeze harder.

I dropped him. He fell like a sack of dirt.

"You'll never stop us," he grunted. "No matter how badly you might defeat us here."

I wasn't worried at this point about the long-term defeat of the Terratakers. Just about saving the lives of the governors in the room beyond.

I scanned the hallway, desperate for something, anything, that might delay us.

Two things grabbed my attention.

One I was familiar with.

The other I only knew because of what I was able to read in white letters against a red background. It was a lever. And the instructions plainly told me to: Pull in case of fire.

Kurt was a few feet from the door. He lifted his robot arm to toss the smoke bomb. When the Supreme Governor saw the motion, he stopped speaking.

Once Cannon's observer in the room noticed the robot at the door, Cannon would begin unplugging them!

I was down to less than 10 seconds. Spinning over to the side of the wall, I pulled as instructed.

Immediately a loud clanging echoed through the building. So loud I could barely hear Ashley. That was good. It meant that anyone trying to get a message to Cannon wouldn't be heard either.

But it was also bad. Because if Cannon didn't pull the plugs, these robots would begin killing the governors who were fighting so hard to help the Earth survive its population explosion.

So I had to stop the robots myself.

But I already had a plan for that. Because of the other fire-related thing that had grabbed my attention. I knew exactly what it would do, because it looked just like the ones at the dome. And I knew exactly what it would do to a robot, because once I'd been beneath one at the wrong time (see *Mission 2: Alien Pursuit*).

"Where's the fire?" Ashley shouted.

I pointed at the ceiling. "There!" Aiming my laser, I shouted the mental command, *Kill!*

An almost invisible red flash of light fired from my finger and burned a hole in the ceiling. I kept firing, and almost instantly the ceiling burst into flame.

I knew what to expect, so I had already pulled Ashley toward a table at the side of the hallway.

"Help me lift!" I shouted above the clanging of the fire alarm. We needed to keep our transmission going so the triangulation could finish. "And stand beneath it with me! This is our umbrella!"

The fire in the ceiling triggered the sprinkler system.

Water burst out of the pipes. And, as the liquid hit the robot bodies below, they began to topple. The water caused their electric currents to short-circuit. When it had happened to me, back on Mars, I'd awakened with nothing worse than a horrible headache. And that was sure better than brain damage.

Water continued to gush downward, pouring off the table Ashley and I used to protect our robot bodies.

The last of the other robots fell around us.

"It's finished," I said to Ashley. "At least for now."

EPILOGUE

Cannon snapped his cell phone shut and turned to me. "They've got Stronsky, but no sign of Dr. Jordan."

"He was communicating with Stronsky by audio," I said. "Even though he left when the countdown was at 15 minutes, if he was in a car he could have been miles away while Stronsky led the robots to the Summit meeting."

"Miles away?" Cannon shook his head. "More if he'd left in a helicopter. By the time we got it all cleaned up, he could have made it to a space shuttle and been halfway into orbit. He was like a ghost commander. Untouchable while he sent his army in."

It had only been eight hours since the robot attack in New York City. Already, it seemed to me like it had never happened. I was in my wheelchair, here in the desert mountains of Parker, Arizona, under a clear blue afternoon sky. It was a world away from the noise and pollution of New York City, where the Combat Force was loading the robot bodies into a truck.

"There's going to be a lot to clean up back there," Cannon said, as if he were reading my thoughts. "Including the Terratakers' penetration of the World United Federation. We knew that some soldiers had turned against us, but all those guards . . ."

I heard Cannon's words, but I was only half listening. My attention had turned to the kids now stepping out into the sunlight. Nate and Ashley had been helping them out of the jelly cylinders while I gave my report to Cannon.

The kids were dressed in clothes that Ashley had found in one of the rooms down a hallway in the Institute. They staggered slightly as they followed Ashley toward the helicopter. I understood why they staggered. I remembered the headache I'd had when my own robot was doused with water back on Mars. And they were probably weak, too, since they'd been in the jelly cylinders for six days, unable to use their own muscles.

Some of the smaller kids, though, found the energy to run and giggle as they pointed to the sky. That, too, I understood. They were free. From their jelly cylinder prison and from Jordan's manipulation.

"Tyce," Cannon began, then stopped as his cell phone rang. "Hang on."

He answered.

I waved at Ashley.

She waved back. One of the bigger kids tapped her on the shoulder. She nodded at him and pointed at me. They both walked straight toward me as Cannon stepped away to speak on his cell phone.

"Tyce," Ashley said as she and the kid neared me in my wheelchair, "this is Kurt."

Kurt smiled, showing straight rows of strong, white teeth. He was much taller than Ashley. With his blond hair smoothed back, he looked like a young movie star. That made me dislike him even more.

"Hey," he said kindly. "Glad to meet you. Ashley tells

me it's true. You *were* born on Mars." He stuck his hand out to shake mine.

I ignored it.

"Tyce?" Ashley frowned. "Don't be like that. Kurt was just trying to protect the other kids. He really couldn't know we were telling the truth when he got them all to unhook our robot computers."

Kurt held his hand out, keeping his smile in place.

"I've got no problem with that," I snapped back. "But ask him about his little deal with Dr. Jordan."

"Deal?" Kurt arranged his face into a puzzled expression.

"Helping out Dr. Jordan so you could be released earlier."

"I doubt it," Kurt said. But his smile now became uncertain.

"I don't."

"Tyce," Ashley said soothingly, "are you sure? You two didn't get off to the best of starts and—"

She stopped. My face felt like it was set in stone as I stared at her. She saw the anger in my eyes. She knew I was telling the truth. I'd tell her all of it later.

"Oh," she said. She took a small step away from Kurt and a step closer to me. She rested her hand on my arm as I continued to speak. "The triangulation worked," I said. "It located 10 other pods, and the Federation immediately sent jets with soldiers to each location. From what I've learned from Cannon, there has been no resistance. All the kids are being rescued as we speak."

"That's good news," Kurt said, trying to get back into the conversation. "Boy, if it wasn't for you . . ."

He didn't notice that Ashley was looking at him as if he were covered with dead skunk.

"What I'm getting at," I continued, speaking to Ashley,

"is that the general has already talked about letting the kids spend a few months with their parents, then sending any of the families who volunteer to Mars. For two reasons. Once all of this makes the news, people on Earth will see them as the soldiers that Dr. Jordan tried to make them. And with all of us able to work our robots on the surface of Mars, we can speed up the settlement project by decades."

"Good, good," Kurt said smoothly. "Count me in."

"Not a chance," I retorted. I turned my head and spoke to Ashley. "The general has already asked me if I'll take a leadership position among all of us who can handle robots. Which I've accepted. And that means my first request is that Kurt does not go to Mars. In fact, when I told the general about Kurt and Dr. Jordan, Cannon said he'd make sure that Kurt never handles another robot as long as he lives."

Finally Kurt's smile faltered. He tried to speak, but Cannon interrupted. "Tyce, Ashley."

I rolled away, and Ashley followed.

"All of the units have reported successful missions," Cannon said. "Out of the 10 pods, nine were similar to this. Kids in jelly cylinders."

"The tenth?" I asked.

"Empty." Cannon said. He let out a breath. "And they still haven't found Chad. Or Brian. They're somewhere, with that missing pod."

He put his hand on Ashley's shoulder. "We're going to do our best to find your parents for you. And the same with Tyce's father. But I may need your help over the next few weeks. Both of you."

"Sir?" I said. All I wanted was to find my father.

"Early indications have given us a hint of where that pod might be." He paused. "Will the two of you go to the Moon?"

IS IT RIGHT TO
MANIPULATE LIFE?

That's the very question Tyce Sanders has been asking himself all through this Mission. After all, the evil Dr. Jordan is totally controlling the jelly kids' lives, treating them as his slaves. He considers them valuable only because they are part of a very expensive experiment.

Even more, Tyce discovers that Cannon has manipulated his life too. After all, the general is the guy who pushed for the funds that caused Tyce's surgery as a baby. The surgery that went wrong and caused his legs to be useless. Tyce is angry—and he has reason to be.

Is it right to manipulate life?

Although the Mars Diaries are set in the future, we need to ask ourselves that question now. You don't have to look much farther than the headlines of your newspaper to find out that life is being manipulated *today.* It all started by genetically manipulating things like corn and beans to give farmers better crops. Then scientists figured out the technology to clone sheep (the first one's name was "Dolly"). Recently the genetic material from a jellyfish was successfully implanted into a monkey.

All these things may sound cool, but they could lead to

scary places in the future. Like what's happening at the Institute on Earth in 2040 A.D., where defenseless kids are being implanted with spinal plugs so they can control robots.

In short, scientists are rapidly becoming more and more able to manipulate the building blocks of life. But the debates on whether this is right or wrong and how far we should go lag far behind the scientific advances. In other words, we as humans are learning *how* to do many things before we as a society are able to decide *whether* or not we should do them.

Is it right to manipulate life? *Is* it OK for Dr. Jordan to use the jelly kids as an experiment?

The Terratakers of the Mars Diaries are like those who believe that humans consist of nothing more than complicated arrangements of protein and water. To the Terratakers, then, humans are in control, and they have the right to decide who should live and who should die. Following this philosophy means to people like Dr. Jordan that the "powerful" people can use the "less powerful" people as their slaves. And that the "powerful" people have more value to society than the "less powerful" people, like the jelly kids.

But that's not what Tyce and his parents, Ashley, Nate, and Rawling McTigre believe. As Christians, they believe that God created the world. That he created each human being uniquely, and that all human beings are equally valuable in his eyes. And as the one who created us, he *and only he* should have power over our life and death. Not people like Dr. Jordan who threaten to use death chips to manipulate others through fear.

When you believe in God, you also have to believe that every life—including your own—is valuable. And that it deserves to be treated with respect.

ABOUT THE AUTHOR

Sigmund Brouwer, his wife, recording artist Cindy Morgan, and their daughter split living between Red Deer, Alberta, Canada, and Nashville, Tennessee. He has written several series of juvenile fiction and eight novels. Sigmund loves sports and plays golf and hockey. He also enjoys visiting schools to talk about books. He welcomes visitors to his Web site at www.coolreading.com, where he and a bunch of other authors like to hang out in cyberspace.

SIGMUND BROUWER'S

COOLWRITING SOFTWARE

EXPERT HELP FOR STUDENT WRITERS

Make your computer an awesome writing tool! **coolwriting** software gives you instant help for your stories, poems, and essays. Like a trusted friend with the answers you need, **coolwriting** is there to help with your writing—while you're typing on your computer. You're sure to improve in skill and confidence with **coolwriting**. Why not test it out? There's a free demo on the **coolwriting** Web site:

http://www.coolreading.com/coolwriting

COME INTO THE COOL

mars
DIARIES

are you ready?

Set in an experimental community on Mars, the Mars Diaries feature 14-year-old Tyce Sanders. Life on the red planet is not always easy, but it is definitely exciting. As Tyce explores his strange surroundings, he also finds that the mysteries of the planet point to his greatest discovery—a new relationship with God.

MISSION 1: OXYGEN LEVEL ZERO
Can Tyce stop the oxygen leak in time?

MISSION 2: ALIEN PURSUIT
What attacked the tekkie in the lab?

MISSION 3: TIME BOMB
What mystery is uncovered by the quake?

MISSION 4: HAMMERHEAD
Will the comet crash on Earth, destroying all life?

MISSION 5: SOLE SURVIVOR
Will a hostile takeover destroy the Mars Project?

MISSION 6: MOON RACER
Who's really controlling the spaceship?

MISSION 7: COUNTDOWN
Will there be enough time to save the others?

MISSION 8: ROBOT WAR
Will the rebels succeed with their plan?

MISSIONS 9 & 10 COMING FALL 2002
Discover the latest news about the Mars Diaries.
Visit www.marsdiaries.com